Dad looked up at us with a stunned expression.

"This is very weird," I noted. Nobody else said anything.

Then Dad opened the letter, very, very carefully. A small old-time key fell out, and Jason grabbed it off the floor. Dad pulled out some folded sheets of paper, looked at them a moment, then smiled and looked at us.

"Vangie's right," he said. "This is very weird indeed. Brace yourselves, gang. This letter appears to be a poem." He read:

> "Oh, knowledge is a fleeting thing,
> Possessing such makes one a king. . . .
> But have ye knowledge, heir of mine,
> You shall my hidden treasure find."

"Hidden treasure!" Jason yelped. "Where's the map?"

By Taffy Cannon:

CONVICTIONS: A Novel of the Sixties

Nan Robinson mysteries:
A POCKETFUL OF KARMA*
TANGLED ROOTS*

MISSISSIPPI TREASURE HUNT*

*Published by Fawcett Books

MISSISSIPPI TREASURE HUNT

Taffy Cannon

FAWCETT JUNIPER • NEW YORK

A Fawcett Juniper Book
Published by Ballantine Books
Copyright © 1996 by Taffy Cannon

Library of Congress Catalog Card Number: 95-90728

ISBN 0-449-70450-5

Manufactured in the United States of America

First Edition: March 1996

10 9 8 7 6 5 4 3 2 1

Special thanks to Sally Lynch, way back when, and to Erin Durnan, much more recently.

CHAPTER ONE

Going in, it certainly didn't seem like the sort of summer that would end with a hunt for buried treasure in a sleepy southern town. It seemed more like the sort of summer that might never end at all.

We were flying from Los Angeles to Marshfield, Minnesota, just outside the Twin Cities, for the summer. My little brother, Jason, and I go back there every summer to stay with my dad and his wife, Carolyn. I'm Vangie Bradley, short for Evangeline, a name I truly hate. I'll be fourteen in August and a high school freshman in the fall. Starting high school scares me a little.

Don't get me wrong. It's always great to see Dad, of course. But Marshfield is kind of quiet, and Dad works long hours as the chief administrator of a hospital. A lot of the time we're pretty much stuck. Carolyn tries, but you can tell she's never spent much time around kids. Besides, she works, too.

Our pilot was one of the chatty ones, always making sure we knew our exact altitude to the half inch, pointing out Broken Zipper, Nebraska, just off to the left of the aircraft, identifying every single one of Minnesota's Ten Thousand Lakes. Now it was time for the weather report.

"We're passing over beautiful country here, no doubt about it," the pilot said. "We're beginning our descent into the Twin Cities now, and we'll be turning on the seat belt sign in just a minute. It's a balmy sixty-seven degrees in Minneapolis–St. Paul right now, with a chance of thundershowers tonight."

Beside me, Jason looked up from his skateboarding magazine. "All right!" he announced, as if a lot of booming thunder and flashing lightning was something to get excited about. Thunderstorms scare me, particularly those big nasty midwestern ones. Actually, Jason's afraid of thunderstorms, too, but he's eleven, working real hard at being cool.

"Maybe there'll be a tornado, too," I told him hopefully. "The whole neighborhood will be destroyed, and we'll have to go back home." I sighed. "I could be on the beach in Malibu right now."

"Waiting for Larry Turner to walk his Samoyeds?" Jason taunted.

Larry Turner is twenty-two and lives four houses down the beach from my stepfather's mother's house. He has a hit TV show and is so gorgeous it takes my breath away: black hair, green eyes, eyelashes long enough to cause breezes.

2

Jason claims not to be impressed by Larry, and maybe he isn't. But he watches Larry's show, "Wellington's World," every week, and he really likes the dogs. Personally, I think they look ridiculous, covered with all that thick, white fur, tongues always hanging out as they desperately try to cool off. Dogs like that don't belong in Southern California. They belong somewhere like Alaska. Or Minnesota.

"Waiting for a tidal wave to sweep you out to Honolulu," I told him sweetly.

He ignored me. "Think Dad'll be there?"

"He'd better be," I answered darkly. But it wasn't something we could count on. He was just as likely to get tied up by some so-called emergency at the hospital and send Carolyn. Like last year.

Sure enough, when the plane landed neither one of them was there. No big deal, really, but *still.* I looked around uncertainly, and Jason clutched the skateboard he'd insisted on stashing under the airplane seat. There was quite a crowd, most of them with those pale Minnesota complexions that come from having about ten months of winter a year. A few people had sunburns, for variety.

Jason nudged me and cocked his head toward a family of three kids, a baby in a stroller, and a mom. All of them, even the baby, were wearing Groucho glasses with big black bushy eyebrows and protruding noses. "And people say California's crazy," Jason whispered, as a man in a gray business suit got off the plane and the kids ran to meet him. He was wearing Groucho glasses, too.

"Vangie! Jason!" Dad came rushing up through the crowd, late as usual. Carolyn was with him, holding his hand. She gets very possessive when we come to visit.

Jason gave a big whoop, and Dad dropped Carolyn's hand, sweeping us both into a hug. "You kids look great!" Dad told us enthusiastically. "Let me take a look at you." He stepped back and smiled. "Growing like weeds," he announced, as if it were a compliment. Then he frowned. "What'd you do to your hair, Vangie?"

I smiled demurely and raised a hand carefully to the hot pink streak I'd sprayed in that morning. It went up through my bangs and back in one section on the right, kind of like that TV anchorwoman with the white streak. The pink matched my shorts and my long, dangly earrings.

"It's an accent, Dad," I explained. This could get interesting. Mom and my stepfather, Nicholas, have been very patiently ignoring the colored streaks I spray in lately, letting me *express myself*, as Nicholas would say. He's a therapist. Of course, I couldn't do it for school, because my junior high had a dress code, of all things. Maybe next year, at the high school, I can get away with it.

"Temporary, I trust," Dad said cautiously. He and Carolyn are pretty conservative. As is Marsh-field, Minnesota. But I was prepared to go to war on this one if necessary. Itching for a fight, if you want to know the truth.

"Oh, sure. It washes right out." No point in telling him yet I have nine different colors, something to match just about every outfit I own.

"It's quite striking," Carolyn said, moving forward. She didn't look particularly happy, but she *did* look very pregnant. Tired, too. Her face was puffy, and her stomach stuck out a mile. The baby's due in September. "Hi, guys."

Jason gave her a mildly enthusiastic hug. Jason is kind of like Larry Turner's dogs in that respect. He'll be friendly to anybody.

"How lovely to see you again," I told Carolyn carefully. I had considered, coming in on the plane, offering her my hand to shake, but at the last minute I chickened out. Dad would think that was bratty, and he'd be right. So I just stood there, hands at my sides. Let Carolyn make the first move if she wanted a hug.

Apparently she didn't. She gave a kind of cock-eyed smile. "Welcome back, Cinderella."

Coming to Marshfield stirs up a lot of emotions in me. I was born here, in St. Paul. But my first memories are all of Los Angeles, where the hospital chain Dad works for sent him as an assistant administrator. Mom immediately fell in love with Southern California, but Dad always hated it. So after their divorce, when he had a chance to go back to Minnesota, he jumped at it, even though he says it half killed him to leave me and Jason behind.

People were all over the place when we pulled into the driveway at Dad's house. One thing about Marshfield, you don't have any trouble figuring out who lives there. All summer long there'd be people around: kids riding bikes, fat men mowing lawns, moms with babies in the park down at the corner.

Jason had a bunch of kids to hang out with, but there wasn't really anybody my age in the immediate neighborhood. I generally don't mix much in Marshfield. The truth is, I don't fit in very well here, and when I was younger, that kind of bothered me. It would be nice to have a friend here, so I wouldn't feel quite so lonely. But I don't, and that's the way it goes.

Dad calls me a loner and maybe he's right, but what's wrong with liking to be by yourself? And right now, I kind of like being a little different. I patted the pink streak in my hair with satisfaction.

"You smuggling gold, Vangie?" Dad asked as he unloaded the luggage. We were traveling heavy, and most of it was mine. Jason had a big duffel bag full of shorts and T-shirts. I had brought four suitcases and a garment bag.

"You need a new joke book, Dad," I told him, picking up the garment bag.

Carolyn went up the front steps, pulled the mail out of the mailbox, and unlocked the door. Inside, everything was about the same. A lot of old furniture with carved wood, fussy pillows, tapestried upholstery, old-fashioned oil paintings of fruit bowls. Not at all like Mom's house in California, which is all open and light and modern.

"You're in the guest room upstairs as usual, Vangie," Carolyn told me, as Jason and Dad staggered in, making a big production out of carrying the bags. "And you're on the screened porch, Jason, if that's okay. Your dad thought you'd prefer it."

Dad smiled. "One of my favorite summer memories when I was a kid was sleeping—"

Jason and I looked at each other and grinned. In unison, we finished Dad's sentence. "—out on the porch with the wind rustling through the trees on the shores of Lake Winnetonka."

We all laughed then. Jason, shuffling his feet, looked casually toward the back screened porch. "So, uh, Dad where's the baby gonna sleep?" Trust Jason not to beat around the bush.

Carolyn sat down, mildly flustered. "Why, we haven't given it much thought. Maybe we'll make the guest room into a nursery."

Jason turned to me, smirking. "Guess you'll be pitching a tent out back next year, Vange." He looked sideways at Dad, acting nonchalant. "So, are we still gonna come summers after the baby's born?" Jason loves these trips. I, on the other hand, was kind of hoping the baby's birth might shorten the summer visits a little. Two months can be a *very* long time.

"Of course you are!" Dad said heartily. He clapped his arm around Jason's shoulders. Jason looked a little relieved, but not entirely convinced. Carolyn was examining her fingernails, which, as always, were kind of chewed-up and ratty-looking.

"I sure hope it's a boy," Jason announced. "I'd love to have a brother."

I smirked at him. "You only say that 'cause you've never had one."

Dad clapped his hands. "Hey! Time out, guys! Grandpa should be here any minute. Let's get these bags upstairs, and then maybe you can help me start the charcoal, Jason. You still in your pyro phase?"

"Absolutely!" Jason answered. It's something he has in common with Mom's husband, Nicholas. When we all went camping over spring break, the two of them built a fire that would have made Joan of Arc very nervous.

"I hope you remembered that I don't eat meat anymore," I told Carolyn.

"Of course we did, dear. I have a soyburger for you. How long have you been a vegetarian, anyway?"

"Since somebody told her meat gives you more zits," Jason said. Brat. In the old days, at least we'd been allies coming here for summers. Now I couldn't count on any kind of support from him.

"*Jason!*" I turned to Carolyn. "That's not true. I just don't want any poor, innocent animals to die on my account." My friend Jennifer has the most

8

horrible video of what happens in slaughterhouses, and since I saw it last March, not one speck of animal flesh has passed my lips.

"Then I hope you sent proper condolences to the mother of your luggage," Dad said. It was easy to see where Jason got his brattiness. And it wasn't like I *chose* that leather luggage anyway. They were Nicholas's mother's old suitcases, and she'd absolutely forced them on me. "C'mon, Jase, let's get the remains of these poor, innocent creatures upstairs."

Jason cocked an ear to the bag at his feet. "This one's still whimpering, Dad."

If I ever get married and have children, I'll *never* get divorced. It's just too awful, and I wouldn't want my kids to go through the terrible sadness I've felt. When Mom and Dad first split up, I cried for months.

I have to admit that Mom and Dad have really been pretty good about everything. A lot of my friends have divorced parents, and some of them have a terrible time. Their parents still fight, and the kids are practically forced to take sides. Or they get stuck with goofy visitation schedules that are impossible for everybody. I really feel sorry for Jennifer. Her mom's been married three times, and her dad four. She's got all kinds of stepbrothers and stepsisters, some of whom she's never even met. Brianne's had a hard time, too. Her mom is pretty young, and she just married a guy who's only twenty-one.

Both my stepparents are okay, I suppose. Of course, Nicholas always wants to know how I *feel* about things, and a lot of the time I don't think it's any of his business. And Carolyn is . . . well, she's just Carolyn, and I can't do anything about it. I guess all that really matters is that Mom and Dad both seem pretty happy now, and when they were married they used to fight all the time.

But I still wish, deep inside me, that none of it had ever happened, that Mom and Dad and Jason and I all still lived together. Happily ever after, whatever that means.

When I got downstairs and went outside, I found that Carolyn had lit a bunch of citronella candles on stakes in the yard. The mosquitoes didn't seem to notice. There were billions of them, more than ever before, thick in the air. Maybe it's kind of a pain to worry about wasting water in Southern California droughts, but at least there isn't standing water everywhere. Every one of Minnesota's ten thousand lakes is a health hazard.

Jason patrolled the barbecue with a squirt gun while a bunch of sausages sizzled. *Sausages*, for heaven's sake, filled with who knows what. And if he didn't get those flames under control, my poor soyburger would taste like one of those charcoal briquets.

Carolyn lay in a rope hammock reading *Baby*

World, in case somebody hadn't gotten the message, and Dad was inside. Just when I thought I'd expire of boredom, a familiar whistle floated up the driveway.

Grandpa Bradley! Jason spun around at the sound, too.

Grandpa is a pretty amazing guy. He's very easygoing and cheerful, and I've never heard him yell at anybody. He has a full head of silver hair and bright blue eyes, which make him look like one of Santa's relatives, maybe a cousin or something. He was wearing outrageous plaid Bermuda shorts, a knit shirt, and sandals with socks. A lot of men wear sandals with socks in Marshfield.

Grandpa smiled and the whole yard lit up.

"Say, do I smell California raisins?" he asked. "Or is that Vangie's latest cologne?"

I jumped up to hug him. Jason beat me there, and the three of us held on to each other tightly, maybe a little longer than necessary. The first thing I always think of now when we see Grandpa is that we aren't going to be able to see Grandma, and I'm sure that's always on his mind, too. She died two years ago, and I miss her.

"You're a fine one to talk about cologne," I told him fondly. He always smells of Old Spice aftershave. Sometimes in the drugstore at home, I'll open a bottle and sniff, just to get a sense of him.

Grandpa stepped back. "Evening, Carolyn. You know, a man couldn't ask for a finer family." He narrowed his twinkling eyes. "That hairstyle have a name, Vangie?"

"She calls it Mervin," Jason announced.

Grandpa leaned down and pulled a can of soda out of the cooler. "Just as much of a smart aleck as your dad, you know that?"

Jason bowed formally. "He's a tough act to follow, Grandpa, but he always says he got it from you."

Grandpa laughed and turned to Carolyn. "You show Jason the whatchamajigger yet?"

Carolyn shook her head and wiped sweat off her forehead with the back of her hand. It was pretty humid, and she looked fairly miserable. "I wanted to wait for you, Ed."

Grandpa looked at Jason. "Could you do me a favor, son, and just reach inside the side door of the garage, without looking, and press the garage door opener?"

Jason obligingly stuck his hand inside the door, pushed the button, then raced back to watch the wooden door lift. It swung up slowly, revealing an enormous wooden skateboard ramp. Jason yelped and raced over to admire it. "Wow, Grandpa, this is really great! Thanks!" He began dragging the ramp onto the driveway.

"Just don't break any bones or I'll never hear the end of it from your father." Grandpa looked around. "Where *is* Ron, anyway?"

"Calling the hospital, surprise, surprise," Carolyn said in a snippy voice.

I looked down at my forearm, where a mosquito the size of a bald eagle was engorged with blood. *My* blood. I slapped it furiously and left a disgusting red and black streak. "I'm being eaten alive! It's never this bad at home."

Grandpa shrugged and handed me a bottle of insect repellent, the kind that smells like a toxic waste dump. "Your average mosquito isn't tough enough to survive the L.A. air. Slather up, girl." He looked past me. "Evening, son."

Dad was coming out the back door. He'd changed to jeans and a casual shirt and was carrying an open letter. He looked stunned, like he'd just been hit by a bus. "Oh, hi, Dad," he said absentmindedly.

"What's the matter, honey?" Carolyn asked anxiously.

Dad wandered over to the picnic table, set the letter down, and sat. This was very strange. "Carolyn," he said, "would you still love me if I were very wealthy?"

I looked at him skeptically. Hospital administrators don't get rich. If Dad had said that once, he'd said it a thousand times. Probably a lot more than a thousand, actually. I could remember him saying it back when he and Mom were still married.

Carolyn smiled, looking confused. "I suppose I could try. Why?"

Grandpa shook his head. "Crime wouldn't suit you, son."

"What's going *on?*" Jason asked.

Dad reached down in the cooler and pulled out a beer. Carolyn got up out of the hammock, no small accomplishment, and came over to pick up the letter. She scanned it quickly as we all watched. Then she looked up and spoke slowly.

"It's a letter from a lawyer in Prestonburg, Mississippi, Jason. It seems your father has inherited the estate of somebody named Griselda Patterson. Ron, who on earth is that?"

CHAPTER TWO

Grandpa laughed so hard that he choked, and Jason had to bang him on the back. When he finally recovered, he shook his head.

"Madeline's loony aunt! Why, I haven't thought about that old nutcase in years." Grandpa turned to Dad. "I wouldn't quit my job just yet, son. Her estate's likely to be two buggy whips and a birdcage. You never told Carolyn about your great-aunt Griselda?"

By now I remembered, too. Vaguely. I smiled at Carolyn, pleased for once to know something that she didn't, to share something with Dad that his new wife wasn't part of. I can be very petty. "Wasn't she the one you sent the pictures to, Dad?"

"Yep. I *thought* I told you kids about her."

Jason looked hurt. "You never told *me* anything."

Dad leaned forward and ruffled Jason's hair. Jason looked embarrassed. "You were probably too young to remember." Well, that was true enough. It was five years now since Mom and Dad's divorce, four since Dad moved back to Minnesota, three since he'd married Carolyn. "Let's get those sausages off the fire and I'll tell you all about Aunt Griselda while we eat. Your grandpa's the one you should really ask, though. He knew her better than I did."

While Dad took the food off the grill, Grandpa disagreed. "Never laid eyes on the woman. Did hear her voice once, though. Your Grandma Madeline and I stopped on our way to Florida. It was while you lived in California, Ron, as I recall."

"You went to her house?" Jason asked.

"Right to the front door," Grandpa answered. "This cackly little voice said she hadn't seen any family since 1938 and wasn't going to start now. That was that. The woman was as nutty as any fruitcake the good ladies down at St. Olaf's ever sold at the Christmas bazaar. Let's get this food on the table, now, and I'll tell you what I do know."

By the time the table was set and everybody was served, the atmosphere was a lot more relaxed. As I'd feared, my soyburger was ruined, though I smiled politely and said it tasted great. Actually, I don't really like soyburgers at all. Back when I ate meat, cheeseburgers were about my favorite food in the world. And if you're not going to eat a real one, it almost doesn't seem worth bothering.

"Aunt Griselda was the last survivor of a southern branch of your Grandma Madeline's family,

16

kids," Dad explained, "and nobody up here knew her. But for some strange reason, she took a special interest in me."

Grandpa dished out some more coleslaw. It's a favorite of mine, Grandma's recipe with raisins in it. I wonder what Carolyn would think if she knew Mom still makes it, too. "Every Christmas for the first twenty-one years of your father's life, she sent him a hundred dollars."

"Wow! That was a lot of money back then, wasn't it?" Despite myself, I was impressed.

"It still is," Carolyn noted irritably. She has this idea that Jason and I are hopelessly spoiled and don't understand the meaning of money. It's one of her more annoying themes.

Dad shot Carolyn a look that almost was a glare. This was always a danger zone. "To 'earn' the money," he went on, "each year I had to send Aunt Griselda a current photograph and a letter about my life."

Jason looked puzzled. "That's all?"

Dad grimaced. "It wasn't that easy, Jason. Writing the letters was murder. My mom insisted that every detail be perfect. Sometimes I had to copy them over three or four times."

"Your Grandma Madeline was a perfectionist," Grandpa agreed fondly. "Me, I was the photo department. Every year by Thanksgiving, I had to drag your daddy into the photo studio at Sears. Five-by-sevens, they had to be. One year there was some kind of mix-up, and I got an eight-by-ten.

Griselda sent the picture back and stopped payment on her check."

Carolyn shook her head in wonder. "I can't believe you two never told me this. I always thought your family was so very ordinary," she said in a hurt voice. "No offense."

"It just never came up, honey." Did Dad have to sound so apologetic? "Besides, the whole thing stopped when I turned twenty-one."

"How come?" Carolyn asked.

"Who knows? The woman's elevator barely reached the mezzanine."

"Actually, what happened," Grandpa said, "was, she sent a letter to Madeline and thanked her and said no further communication would be required. That would be . . . how long ago, Ron?"

"Seventeen years, Dad. Thanks for the reminder." Ever since my dad's hair started thinning, he's gotten very self-conscious about his age. I'd already checked out the new NordicTrack in the basement. Which Carolyn made a point of saying they'd gotten secondhand, which is something she knows a *lot* about. Carolyn runs this really goofy gift consignment store, kind of a cross between a thrift shop and the world's worst souvenir stand. It's full of stuff like gold-plated toothpick dispensers and shish-kabobbers and combination shoe buffer/lawn clippers.

"Always happy to share the aging process, son," Grandpa told him cheerfully. "The letter says they'd like you to go down there. When can you do that?"

"Can I come too?" Jason asked. Was he serious?

Dad looked around the table and considered. "We're supposed to go to the lake for two weeks at the Fourth of July. I could go to Mississippi then, while the rest of you are at the lake."

"But I want to go, too!" Jason protested.

"So do I," Carolyn announced, surprising me for a moment. Then I realized that there was money involved, at least the possibility of *getting* money. She frowned. "Would it be too terribly expensive if we all went to Mississippi and then went to the lake?"

This must be, I realized glumly, what was meant by having a choice between the frying pan and the fire. Being at the lake with a pregnant Carolyn while Dad was gone would be awful, but the idea of visiting Mississippi seemed even worse. *Mississippi*, for heaven's sake. It might as well be Afghanistan.

"Can we, Dad? Can we?" Jason was practically jumping up and down.

Dad nodded his head. "I suppose anybody who specifically requests a trip to Prestonburg, Mississippi, deserves to have their wish granted. Sure. Why not?"

And so it happened that the four of us climbed down the steps of the world's tiniest commercial airliner at the Prestonburg-Waynesville Airport two weeks later on a sweltering Mississippi afternoon.

I blinked in astonishment. For one thing, I'd never been on an airport tarmac before. All the planes I've ever taken boarded through jet-ways, leading you straight from the terminal into the cabin, with just a little hint at the door of the plane that there was cement way down below. But this tiny airport, with its bitsy little prop jets and roll-up stairway—it was like something out of an *Early Days of Aviation* picture book.

And it was *hot*, too. Hot enough that everything almost looked black and white. Steamy, sticky hot. I could actually see heat rising off the tarmac, and the humidity was unbelievable. Carolyn and Dad were right behind me, and I could see Carolyn wilting. Jason, of course, was unfazed. He plopped down his skateboard and rode off toward the terminal, a miniature building a hundred yards away.

Inside we were greeted by a welcome blast of air-conditioning. The terminal building was almost empty, with just a few rows of chairs and a couple of airline and car-rental counters across the room. Not very many people had gotten off the plane, and only one of them was met by anybody. So much for that famous Southern hospitality.

Carolyn collapsed into a chair. "This heat is *horrendous*! You three get the car and send a litter for me."

"C'mon, kids," Dad told us, striding off to the car-rental counter.

The woman at the counter was very pretty, with beautiful shoulder-length blond hair and quite a lot of makeup, very nicely applied. It gave her a kind of formal look, as if she were in a beauty contest or something. And her accent! It was so thick that I could barely understand her, but she lit right up when she heard Dad's name.

"Mr. Bradley," she told him with an extra-big smile, "it took a little doing on your special order, but we managed to obtain just the car you requested."

Special order? *Dad?*

Dad grinned and gave a thumbs-up to Jason and me, then started all the rigmarole of paperwork, without giving any hint what he was up to. No problem. We had all the time in the world. And when we went back out in the sweltering heat to the lot and found the car, I finally understood. Maybe Dad still had a little spark left in him after all.

He'd ordered a white Cadillac limousine, all bright and waxed and shiny. It wasn't a stretch limo like the kids at school get for special occasions, but *still*. Old penny-pinching Carolyn, I thought with almost embarrassing satisfaction, was going to split a gut.

I thought the surprises were over, but as we brought the car up to the front of the terminal, our luggage arrived on a small, motor-driven cart. A man unloaded our stuff and a few other bags onto a platform beside the terminal. The platform and bags just sat there. No carousel, no conveyor belts, nothing but plain old heaving and lifting. Nobody checking baggage tag numbers, either. I guess they weren't worried about theft at the Prestonburg-Waynesville Airport.

Carolyn surprised me, too. She didn't get mad at all about the limo. When Jason ran inside to bring her out, I leaned back in the backseat and smiled, anticipating fireworks. For just a moment Carolyn looked angry, but then her eyes crinkled, and a moment later she was laughing out loud.

"Ron," she said between major spasms of laughter, "this is positively outrageous. What *fun!*"

Dad beamed at her and held the front passenger door open. "Your chariot, madame. I figure, how often does one fall heir to an old Southern fortune, anyway?"

"Not nearly often enough," Carolyn replied with an arched eyebrow, as she stepped elegantly across the sidewalk and took Dad's hand to get into the car.

Then we were off. Jason kept craning his neck, but as far as I could tell there wasn't much to see. The airport was midway between Prestonburg and Waynesville, which were both midway between Nowhere and Oblivion.

We were passing through thick woods, impossibly green and overgrown with strange vines that Dad identified as kudzu. Kudzu, he said, would grow six feet in a single day under the right circumstances. And there are no wrong circumstances in this Mississippi climate, which it adored. At one point we passed an abandoned house that was completely covered with vines. You could barely tell what had been underneath to start with. And a lot of the power and phone lines were overrun with the stuff. It was like something out of a science fiction movie.

Finally we came to a sign:

WELCOME TO PRESTONBURG
THE FRIENDLY LITTLE CITY
POPULATION 7452

Just below it a smaller sign pointed down a side road:

CHINATAW MOUND—2 MILES

Jason had been wiggling for the past couple of miles. Now he piped up, "Uh, Dad? Do they have bathrooms in Prestonburg?"

Dad looked back and smiled wickedly. "Maybe." I wasn't betting on it, myself.

The gas station we pulled into on the outskirts of town had to be forty years old. On one side was a faded sign for Sinclair Gasoline. I know for a fact that brand hasn't even existed since before I was born, because on the way to Palm Springs there's this place with a big Sinclair dinosaur, and Nicholas told me all about it.

Out front there were a couple of dilapidated

pumps, and as we pulled in, two men came out of the open garage. Jason jumped out and trotted around the corner of the building. When Dad got out, the mechanics came over, frankly staring. The older one wore a uniform with his name on the shirt—Dave—and the younger one, who was actually kind of cute, had on tight jeans and a greasy T-shirt. He was probably about eighteen and had short, dark hair and lazy brown eyes.

"Now whadda we got here?" Dave, the old mechanic, wondered aloud. I guess we looked as alien to them as they did to us. To me, anyway. "A rock band, maybe?"

I stepped out of the car and stretched, feeling surprisingly bold. The cute young mechanic was checking me out, particularly staring at my hair. Today's stripe was chartreuse, and the matching earrings were plastic circles the size of silver dollars.

"Nobody I ever seen before," the young one said, giving me a wink. I wasn't entirely sure whether to be flattered or insulted.

Dad spoke up. "Could you tell me how to get to Amos Winthrop's office?"

The mechanics looked at each other, jolted by surprise. "Miss Griselda's nephew!" said Dave.

"You know who I am?" Dad sounded stunned.

The mechanic gave a chuckle. "I reckon just about everybody in the county knows y'all're expected. How can we help y'all? Gasoline? Under the hood? Co'-Cola?"

Dad wiped sweat from his brow. "The car's okay, but *I'm* overheated. Something cold sounds tempting."

Dave pointed at an ancient red Coke machine. Dad went over and lifted the lid, then gave a glorious grin. Moments later he was holding four six-ounce Coke bottles. With a flourish, he presented one to each of us. He was getting downright courtly in this environment. Very weird.

As were the Cokes.

"It's so cold, it's slushy!" Carolyn remarked, surprised.

"Neat little bottles," Jason approved.

I shook my head in disbelief. "So is this one of those things left over from the olden golden days, Dad, that you're always telling us about?"

Dad chuckled and looked around the gas station. Dave had disappeared, but the younger guy was watching from inside the garage, on the far side of a pickup truck with the hood up. Acting cool, like he wasn't watching, but eyeballing us pretty steadily. I was secretly pleased.

"I have a feeling, kiddo," Dad said, "that this whole town is going to fit that description. The question is, *which* olden golden days?"

CHAPTER
THREE

The lawyer's office wasn't an office at all.

It was a house, an old two-story wooden building painted pale yellow with white shutters and trim. An inviting white wooden double swing hung on the wide porch, and some pretty shrubs bloomed on either side of the front walk. The lawn was a rich deep green, perfectly manicured, and in the absolute center on one side of the walk, a simple wooden sign announced: WINTHROP & SONS, ATTORNEYS AT LAW.

Not exactly Century City, where lawyers work by the thousand in shiny towers. Mom's divorce lawyer had been in one of the Delta Towers, almost on the top floor. I remember looking out the windows all the way to Catalina Island when I was about eight. Everything in that office was ultra-modern glass and chrome.

As we got out of the car, I had the feeling that people were watching. I couldn't see anybody looking at me—or any of us—and it was far too hot for anyone with any sense to be outside anyway. But still I felt observed, and it made me a bit uneasy.

The reception area inside was full of antiques—the kind that had Carolyn making little *ooh*ing noises immediately, starting with a breakfront and matching desk in some dark reddish wood, polished to a deep warm glow. There were lace curtains on the front window, and a big ceiling fan was really pumping away. There must have also been air-conditioning, though, 'cause it was a lot cooler inside than on the porch, which had felt like about a hundred and thirty degrees.

The young woman at the desk had pretty blue eyes, soft and opaque like Indian turquoise. But her dress! It was hideously dowdy, in a ballpark mustard shade that was terrible for her coloring. It made her skin look sallow and took all the life out of her hair, which was very fine and a probably natural silver-ash-blond shade.

Maybe they hadn't heard of doing your colors down here, even though the rest of the world has been doing it forever. I was seven when Mom first did mine. I'm a Summer, which is great because it lets me use really vivid colors for the streaks in my hair. Today's chartreuse perfectly matched my shorts. Carolyn was not pleased when she first saw my traveling outfit, and I could tell that Dad was biting his tongue, too. But neither of them had specifically mentioned it.

The receptionist jumped to her feet. "Why, you just *have* to be the Bradleys," she drawled in a honeyed voice. It sounded almost like a foreign language. It was not going to be easy to communicate down here. The only southerners I'd ever heard were in the movies. "Welcome to Prestonburg."

I smiled sweetly at her. She kept staring at the streak in my hair, then realizing it was rude to stare and glancing away.

A man in a wrinkled, pale blue suit had been sitting on the corner of the desk talking to the receptionist when we came in. He was in terrible shape, tubby and kind of flushed as if he'd just run a 5K race. He glanced at each of us, did a fast double take at my hair, then slicked back his own hair—which was black and greasy—and held a hand out to Dad.

"I'm Lee Winthrop, Mr. Bradley. Amos Lee Winthrop the Third, actually," he announced. "It's my granddaddy y'all are here to see. And this lovely lady must be Mrs. Bradley. Could I get you a chair, ma'am?"

Carolyn was already sinking into one of the wing chairs in the waiting room. It was upholstered in antique brocade. "This will be fine for the moment, thanks."

Dad gave Lee Winthrop's hand a hearty shake. "Pleased to meet you. These are my children, Jason and Vangie."

Lee Winthrop stuck his hand out at Jason, who looked at it for a moment in surprise, then glanced at Dad and shook it. He didn't offer a hand to me, which was a shame. I was planning a little curtsy.

The receptionist was already on her way out of the room, scooting toward the back of the house. "I'll just go tell Mr. Amos that y'all are here."

An old and imperious voice came from beyond her. "That won't be necessary, Melanie."

Amos Winthrop stepped into the reception area, and everything suddenly froze. Only the ceiling fan kept moving. Mr. Winthrop was a distinguished-looking silver-haired man in an impeccable cream-colored suit. He looked at the young man, frowning. "Amos Lee, weren't you going to see Judge Carter?"

Lee Winthrop suddenly looked about four years old. He cringed. "On my way, Granddaddy." He turned to Dad. "When I get back, maybe I could just take y'all by Miss Griselda's place and—"

His grandfather interrupted. "The judge has always set a particular store by punctuality."

Lee Winthrop picked up his briefcase and scooted out the door, making one last attempt. "Anything at all I can help with . . ."

The older man ignored him. "Mr. and Mrs. Bradley, I'm Amos Winthrop. Why don't y'all come back into my office now? Perhaps the youngsters would be more comfortable out here."

"Oh, I think they can come along with us," Dad said. Kind of surprising, really. I hadn't expected him to let us in on the good stuff. Of course, there was an excellent chance that this lawyer would be boring beyond belief.

Mr. Winthrop raised an eyebrow. "Very well. Melanie, dear, could you fetch us some cold drinks, please? Mrs. Bradley looks a trifle warm."

Mrs. Bradley actually looked like she was about to pass out from heat prostration. With an effort, Carolyn got up and followed him down the hall. Jason and I brought up the rear.

The old lawyer's office was large and full of more antique furniture. Law books sat behind glass in oak cases, and oil portraits of severe-looking men from bygone eras hung on the walls. On one side of the room, a large window looked out into a rose garden in full bloom. A vase of roses on the desk smelled wonderful.

Back behind his desk, Amos Winthrop seemed to hesitate, uncertain just how to begin. He made a steeple out of his fingers. "Now, let's see. I know from our telephone conversation that Miss Griselda wasn't close to your family, even though you were her nearest kin. So maybe it would help if I just explained a bit about her background. You see, Miss Griselda was a mite, well . . ." His voice trailed off delicately.

"Eccentric?" Dad suggested.

The lawyer nodded, with a smile. "Eccentric. That'll do very nicely, I think. Why, thank you, dear," he said to Melanie, who had come in with a huge tray holding a pitcher and five glasses of iced lemonade. She passed the glasses around shyly, then left with a final backward glance at my hair. Mr. Winthrop, interestingly, never gave the slightest hint that he'd noticed it. Either he was exceptionally polite or his eyes were going.

Mr. Winthrop leaned back. "It all really started with old Langley Patterson and the Wishing Rock Plantation. Now, Langley was born around eighteen and thirty-seven, and he was raised to be a gentleman. Handsome devil, they say he was, and the ladies all loved him. But when the War Against Northern Aggression came, he refused to enlist. Went to New Orleans instead and became a gunrunner for the Confederacy. When the war ended, Langley disappeared, and talk was, he'd made off with the Confederate gold."

Confederate *gold*? We hadn't covered *that* in American history last year, and we spent a solid six weeks on the Civil War.

"Really," murmured Carolyn. She was leaning back in her chair, sipping lemonade, looking fascinated.

"But then," Mr. Winthrop continued, "after ten years or so, he came back and he swore he'd never had the gold at all. The ladies still loved him, and he married a local girl named Ellen. They had three children. Got himself a house here in town and started calling himself a lawyer. Then he opened up a practice here in Prestonburg, in this very building, with my granddaddy." The lawyer indicated a dour-looking fellow with white muttonchop sideburns in one of the portraits on his office wall.

His expression saddened. "But one of Langley's sons got killed in the Spanish-American War, and his daughter died of pneumonia one winter. Then Langley's horse threw him and broke his neck, and his wife died of the shock. Quite a set of calamities, all told. Which left just Langley's son Philip, and Philip wasn't much good at anything."

Amos Winthrop ticked off Philip's deficiencies on his fingers. "Couldn't shoot, bad card player, *terrible* lawyer. 'Bout all he was good at was geology. He was always traveling around, hunting after different rocks. People still wondered about that Confederate gold, but the general consensus was that Philip wouldn't know it if it fell on him.

"He married a little lady from Jackson, name of Susanna, sister to your great-grandmother, Mr. Bradley, and everybody wondered just what it was she saw in him. Never found out, though, 'cause she died in childbirth."

He shook his head. "It was just Philip and baby Griselda, then. Now, Griselda was a pretty little thing, totally devoted to her daddy. She never got married, never left home. Her daddy found fault with all the young fellows who wanted to marry her, and I don't reckon she fought him too hard on it. Before long, she was just another old maid."

Carolyn flinched slightly at that, I noticed. She'd been thirty-two when she married Dad, and this was her first marriage.

"Then in nineteen and thirty-eight, old Philip had a heart attack one Sunday afternoon," Mr. Winthrop continued. "Miss Griselda was heartbroken. She locked herself up in that house and wouldn't come out for anything. Had a lady to come in and clean for her, mute woman named Mary, couldn't talk about what she saw. Anything she needed, she had delivered."

I wiggled a bit restlessly on the love seat I was sharing with Jason. No doubt about it, Amos Winthrop was a natural storyteller, and this was all very nice—maybe even interesting if you wanted to stretch a point. But so what?

"As far as I know," he went on, "the only time she ever left the house was when she came in here one day about thirty-five years ago to draw up her will. Things went on that way till Griselda was well into her eighties."

He leaned forward. "When she died, Mary found her, and they brought her out, but nobody's been in there since. I don't mind telling y'all there's a lot of folks mighty curious about the inside of that house. If y'all'd like, we could go on over there right now."

Dad looked stupefied. He glanced at Carolyn, who gave a little shrug. Why not? Why not indeed, I agreed. The day couldn't get much stranger.

"Sounds fine to me," Dad agreed. He hesitated a moment. "But before we go, could you fill me in on the provisions of my great-aunt's will?"

Mr. Winthrop drained his lemonade with relish

and set the glass down. "More lemonade, anyone? No? Well, Mr. Bradley, the entire estate goes to you. However, Miss Griselda was what you might call cash poor. John Reynolds over at the bank tells me there's a small amount in her account after the funeral expenses, but the main asset is the house. Unless she found the Confederate gold, heh-heh."

Heh-heh indeed, I thought.

CHAPTER FOUR

Miss Griselda's house looked like it might very well be haunted.

The place was about as old as the Winthrop law office, and built in pretty much the same style, but nobody had taken much care of this house for a long time. Paint was flaking and peeling everywhere, and the porch was dirty, with dry leaves in little piles in the corners. Big wooden shutters were closed tightly all over the building, and a giant spiderweb hung over the front door.

I shivered involuntarily as Amos Winthrop turned a key in the front door.

"I've been wanting to see in here for fifty years," Mr. Winthrop said with some satisfaction. Behind him, Jason pushed a porch glider, which gave an awful creak. Carolyn jumped six inches.

We crossed a small, dark foyer and entered the parlor. The place smelled incredibly musty and it was very, very hot. The parlor was jammed with small tables and needlepoint footstools and old-fashioned furniture covered with doilies. Carolyn's idea of heaven.

Mr. Winthrop turned on a fringed table light, revealing a heavy layer of dust on everything.

On the far side of the room stood a large wooden radio, similar to one that my friend Lauren's parents have. I crossed over to it with curiosity and tried to turn it on. Dead as a doornail. Whatever that means.

"Maybe it's full of Confederate gold," Jason suggested. He looked a bit confused. "Just what *is* Confederate gold, anyway?"

I'd been wondering about that myself.

Mr. Winthrop was busy examining a picture on the wall and, for once, had nothing to say. It was Dad who finally spoke up.

"During the Civil War," Dad explained, with a nervous glance at Mr. Winthrop, "the South was short of money. They kept printing more and more paper money, even though that made it all worth less. A lot of people didn't want to believe there was nothing to back that paper money up. They claimed the Confederacy actually had a lot of gold. Somewhere. Nobody knew quite where, though, and it never turned up. Folks liked to claim that it had been stolen."

Dad looked again at Mr. Winthrop, who was still pretending the picture was really interesting. As far as I could see, it was just a couple of hunting dogs. "There's no evidence that the Confederate gold ever existed, Jason," Dad concluded. "But it makes a nice story."

Jason had grown increasingly restless. His attention span is pretty limited. "Humph," he said, then darted down the hall and out of sight. Moments later his voice came from somewhere deep inside the house. "Hey, wow! Come look at this!"

He'd found an old office. It held a massive wooden rolltop desk and shelving on all the walls, floor to ceiling. Every inch of shelf space was covered with rocks, like a science museum. There were hundreds and hundreds of rocks, some quite pretty, others very boring, all neatly labeled in fading ink on yellowed cards.

Dad picked up a huge chunk of glittering pyrite, bigger than his fist. "Here's your Confederate gold, Jason. It's pyrite, fool's gold."

Carolyn had gone straight to the desk, making a small purring noise in her throat. She opened the front gingerly, to reveal dozens of pigeonholes, mostly full of papers. She lovingly caressed the gleaming old wood.

"What a magnificent piece of furniture," she said softly. She turned to Dad. "Ron, just *look* at this beautiful burl. Wouldn't this be great in the living room between the side windows?"

Dad looked at the desk and smiled, putting his arm around her. "You're right, it would. Happy birthday, hon." He turned to Amos Winthrop. "Can you help arrange to ship some things for us?"

Mr. Winthrop was looking at the desk now, too,

though he seemed more interested in the papers inside. "Of course. I should inform you also that the local Historical Society is interested in possibly using this house as a headquarters. They have a place out in the country, but they've been wanting to set up here in town."

Dad brightened. "Do they want to buy the house?" he asked hopefully. I couldn't imagine that he'd want to keep the place. It was a little too creepy, and a million miles away from everything.

Mr. Winthrop shook his head regretfully. "I'm afraid their budget doesn't run to that, and you'll find the real estate market here is a trifle stagnant in any case. There are places in town that have been on the market for years." He smiled brightly. "But I do know the Historical Society would be happy to pay any reasonable rent."

Jason slipped out again as Dad and Carolyn exchanged looks. Carolyn had perked right up when he mentioned that "reasonable rent."

"Could you arrange for us to talk with them?" Dad asked.

"They'll be in my office tomorrow morning at nine," Mr. Winthrop told him with a smile.

Now Jason was calling us again. "Hey, Dad, this water's brown!"

We found him in the kitchen. Here, just about everything was dingy. It was a large, quaint room with a scarred wooden table in the center. The stove and refrigerator looked like they belonged in a museum, but not the same one as the rocks. Jason was running water in the sink.

"It's just rusty pipes, son," Dad told him. "Should clear in a minute."

I opened a door at the side of the room, then recoiled at a massive spiderweb just inside the door. An absolutely *huge* spider sat in the absolute center of it. "Eeeoh! Yuck!"

Jason came running as Carolyn pulled the door open further. Jason knocked down the spiderweb, and the spider went scurrying off behind some of the jars on the shelves inside. It was a pantry, and the strangest one I'd ever seen. There was almost nothing in it but Mason jars, thousands of them. There were a few jars of pickles and tomatoes, but most were labeled OKRA.

"What's okra?" Jason asked, holding up a jar tentatively.

"The most convincing argument I know against vegetarianism," Dad answered. "Ever had okra, Vangie?"

I shook my head as Jason handed me the jar. The vegetables inside were a dull green, about four inches long, half an inch thick at one end and pointed at the other. They weren't long on eye appeal.

"Imagine eating a snail trail," Dad continued. "That's okra. Pure slime." Flesh-eaters are always so smug when they discuss some yucky vegetable, never stopping to think that *anybody* with any sense will hate turnips and brussels sprouts. I was willing to add okra to my personal list of disgusting veggies without even bothering to taste it.

Carolyn abruptly dropped into a chair beside the kitchen table, pulled a baby magazine out of her purse, and started fanning herself. She was very pale, and I suddenly realized how beastly hot it was inside that house. It didn't have air-conditioning, didn't have a fan going, didn't even seem to have windows that opened. As I thought about it, I started to feel a little woozy myself.

Now Jason was back again, returning from the deeper recesses of the okra pantry. He had a tall bottle labeled CHERRY BOUNCE. "What's this? Soda pop?"

Mr. Winthrop chuckled. "It packs a bit more punch than that. That's Cherry Bounce, son. It's a fermented beverage folks around here have always been partial to."

Jason examined the bottle more closely. It was labeled 1963 and seemed to contain the remains of cherries—or something—in the bottom. He experimentally twisted the cap. Suddenly the top exploded, showering him in red liquid.

"Argh!" Jason yelped.

Mr. Winthrop frowned. "That's likely to stain your shirt, son."

Dad licked a drop of Cherry Bounce that had landed on his arm. "Stain nothing," he said. "It's likely to eat a hole in it. This must be two-hundred proof."

"Wouldn't surprise me," Mr. Winthrop agreed cheerfully. "Shall we go upstairs?"

I kept trying not to think about *Psycho* as we climbed the steep narrow stairs. At the top, four closed doors greeted us. Carolyn hesitated, then opened one, revealing a large bathroom. She left the door open and tried a second. This one was dark. Taking a deep breath, she walked in.

It was very masculine, a Man's Room for an old-style man, with a large Confederate flag hanging on one wall over crossed Confederate swords. And spooky, too: the bed was turned down, a man's nightgown and bathrobe were laid out, and a yellowed newspaper lay on the table.

"This must have been Philip's room," Mr. Winthrop said softly. He moved to the bed, touched the dark blue woolen bathrobe.

With no warning whatsoever, Jason pulled one of the swords off the wall and lunged at me. As I shrieked for him to stop, Dad carefully picked up the newspaper.

"March 23, 1938," he read. "This must have all been this way since . . ."

Jason leered, vampire-style, and brandished the sword. This place was bringing out the absolute worst in him. ". . . the night he died," he finished in a "Creature Features" voice.

I turned on a dresser lamp and fingered a silver hairbrush. It was hardly even tarnished. Which had to mean that somebody had regularly *tended* this room, polished the silver, maybe even changed the linens. "This place gives me the heebie-jeebies," I announced to nobody in particular, shuddered, and headed for the door.

The others followed, with Jason humming the "Twilight Zone" theme. "Dee-da-da-da, dee-da-da-da . . ." He thinks he's so cute.

Griselda's room, across the hall, was much nicer. For one thing, the shutters here weren't closed. So it was actually possible to open the curtains and get some real light, which Carolyn did as soon as she came in.

Everything here was fussy and frilly and feminine, with enough lace for a whole issue of *Bride's Magazine*. The wallpaper, pink flowers in formal arrangement, was softly faded. The room had a faint scent of lavender.

A dressing table with a pink ruffled skirt caught my eye immediately. I crossed and sat down, taking a moment to check my hair. Amazingly, it hadn't melted right off my head. The chartreuse streak was looking a little tired, though.

Behind me, in the mirror, I could see Carolyn picking up a lace pillow off the bed. "Why, this lacework is exquisite, Ron! It's all done by hand. If Griselda did this herself, it took years."

But Dad wasn't paying attention. He and Jason stood in front of the opposite wall. Twenty portraits of Dad as a boy hung in neat rows. The frames were elaborate, with lots of curls and whorls, but they didn't match. Some were wood and some were metal, and all they had in common was their size.

"So this is where they all ended up," Dad said thoughtfully.

"You were kind of geeky, you know that, Dad?" Jason told him.

I turned around and looked at the pictures. Jason had a point.

"I favor my son," Dad retorted. "But this is only twenty. Where's the other one?" He looked around the room. "The last one?"

It was right in front of me, sitting on the dressing table in one side of a double silver frame. "Here," I told him. "Next to some other old geezer."

Mr. Winthrop, who'd been kind of shifting his weight by the door, crossed over to look at the picture I was talking about. He smelled of lime. "That's Philip Patterson, Miss Griselda's father," he announced.

"One more room up here," Dad said, "and then I suspect Carolyn would like to get down into a cool breeze. I know I would."

He left the room, and we all followed as he opened the last remaining door.

Wouldn't you know, we'd saved the weirdest for last. I blinked a couple of times, thinking it might get less strange.

It didn't.

The walls and windows were covered by large sheets of embroidered cloth, draped loosely but very formally. As I looked more carefully, I could see that the embroidery featured complicated scenes, complete with people, buildings, dates, and brief descriptions. It told the same tale of the Patterson family history that Amos Winthrop had related in his office an hour earlier.

It was all there: Langley Patterson, Langley's family and their varied demises, Philip's life. One entire panel seemed devoted to the Civil War, which I was not about to call the War Against Northern Aggression, or even the War Between the States, thank you very much. No matter what kind of spin these people wanted to put on history.

At the center, the sheets were draped toward a table holding a large framed portrait of Philip Patterson. The photo was flanked by elaborate candelabra and two large, rather tarnished silver vases filled with dead flowers.

I looked more closely at the man in the picture. He wasn't particularly handsome or ugly or remarkable in any way that showed. He was the kind of guy you could see over and over but never quite remember. Yet Griselda had never married, had given up any chance for a life of her own in order to care for him. She'd even let him control her life after his death, when she holed up in this spooky old house for so many years. And she'd created this bizarre room in his honor.

I couldn't help shuddering. The whole room was unbearably creepy. The whole *house* was unbearably creepy.

Carolyn was checking out the needlework. "This is story embroidery," she explained, "and it's all handwork, too. I can't believe Griselda never showed this to anybody. She must have worked on it for decades."

"A ridiculous waste of time," I snorted. Let me *out* of here!

Mr. Winthrop shook his head reproachfully at me. "It's a shrine, that's what it is, young lady. And a history lesson at the same time." He pointed to various sections of the embroidery. "Here's the settling of Prestonburg, and the war, and the whole Patterson family story."

Just then a sharp knock came from downstairs.

CHAPTER FIVE

The two little old ladies standing in the foyer talking to Mr. Winthrop were practically quivering with excitement. As I came downstairs, I could see them craning their delicate necks in every direction. They wore similar dresses, pale floral prints with white lace collars, and sensible white shoes. They looked and acted like fluffy-haired little birds.

"Mr. and Mrs. Bradley," Mr. Winthrop said formally, "may I present the Misses Tuthill. Miss Lavinia and Miss Estelle are your neighbors across the street here."

Miss Lavinia, who was taller and wore glasses with little rhinestones in the corners, carefully handed Carolyn a chocolate cake. It was spectacularly frosted and stood a good six inches tall. "We wanted to welcome y'all to Prestonburg, Miz Bradley."

Miss Estelle kept shifting her weight, like a little kid anxious to find the bathroom. "We were so distraught when poor, dear Griselda passed on, Mr.

Bradley," she simpered. "Such a lovely woman, and so devoted to her late father." That was putting it mildly, it seemed to me. Miss Estelle turned to Mr. Winthrop. "Will we be meeting in the morning, Amos?"

Mr. Winthrop nodded.

"Why, that's wonderful!" Miss Lavinia enthused. Her drawl was even thicker than her sister's. We could have used a simultaneous translator, like they have at the United Nations so that people speaking Chinese can be understood by, say, the Germans. Except for us it would be English to English. "Mr. Bradley, the Historical Society is so hopeful we can make an arrangement with y'all . . ."

"Let's leave these good people be for the present, Lavinia," Mr. Winthrop suggested. He spoke just as slowly as everybody else, but his words had real force behind them, as if people generally took his suggestions. Without a lot of back talk.

But Miss Estelle moved a little closer to him, cocking her head and batting her eyelashes. Batting her eyelashes?

"I don't suppose there's any chance we might take a teeny-tiny little peek around, Amos?" Miss Estelle entreated.

Mr. Winthrop shook his head firmly. "Tomorrow, Estelle, tomorrow. And then only if Mr. Bradley wishes. Ladies, if y'all'd excuse us, I was about to take the Bradleys over to Mildred Farnsworth's Bed-and-Breakfast."

Which was, I realized glumly, probably yet another version of this place and the law office. It was probably too much to hope that there'd be a TV anywhere. Tonight was "Wellington's World," starring Larry Turner. Oh, well. At least I'd thought to bring my Walkman.

As Mr. Winthrop walked the Tuthill sisters outside, with a firm hand on Miss Estelle's elbow, Jason tugged on Dad's sleeve.

"Dad, I don't want to go to that dumb bed-and-breakfast place," Jason told him, not quite whining but right on the borderline. "How about if we stay here tonight?"

"Eeyuck!" It popped out before I realized. This place was full of spiders and dirt and weird memories and, for all we knew, ghosts. "No way!"

Carolyn shook her head adamantly. "It's too hot here, Jason."

Jason held his hands up. "Well, how about if I stay here by myself, then? C'mon, Dad, can I?"

Dad looked at him thoughtfully. "Son, it's not that I don't trust you, but somehow eleven doesn't seem quite old enough to spend the night alone in a strange house in a strange town." Disappointment poured over Jason's face, but then Dad grinned slyly. "On the other hand, if you were to stay here with a responsible adult, me for instance . . ."

"You must be joking," Carolyn said flatly. She was sitting down again, just inside the parlor, fanning herself with the baby magazine.

Dad squatted beside her chair. "No, honey, listen. I know we've already paid for the rooms, but you and Vangie can stay there and we'll meet you for breakfast in the morning. Tell the truth, I think it sounds like fun to stay here." He looked at her with the same puppydog expression Jason always used on Mom when he didn't think he'd get his own way.

And it worked.

"Well," Carolyn said slowly, "I suppose . . . Vangie?"

So it was up to me, was it? Leave them to the spiders if they were so determined. I shrugged. "Whatever."

Dad turned to Mr. Winthrop, who had just returned from ushering the Tuthill sisters off the grounds. "Mr. Winthrop, Jason and I have decided to sleep here tonight."

Mr. Winthrop raised an eyebrow. It looked like a thick white caterpillar. "I should warn you," he said slowly. Even more slowly than usual. "You'll be besieged by the curious. Neighbors bearing an endless procession of baked goods. The Tuthill sisters and their cake are just the first float in what's likely to be a mighty long parade. As a matter of fact, my sister Clara should be by any minute with a pecan pie."

"That's okay," Dad said with a grin. "We're tough."

That night, after a fried chicken dinner at a little restaurant where everybody fussed over us, I decided to stay at the bed-and-breakfast while the others went back to Griselda's house. It was starting to cool off a little, and I needed some time by myself.

I thought about calling Mom, using the telephone credit card Nicholas had given me, but I wasn't sure what I'd say to her. I was far too confused by all that had happened since we stepped off the plane. And I didn't want to try to explain to Nicholas how I *felt*.

Besides, I'd just talked to Mom last night. She sounded happy enough, talking about the summer school classes she's teaching, but I could tell she's really missing us. She always tries to be very chipper when we talk, but her voice usually cracks at the end when she says, "I love you." So does mine.

I got out the little leather-bound copy of *Evangeline* that she gave me right before we left for Minnesota. It has gold edges on the pages and was published over a hundred years ago. It's the nicest book I've ever owned, as well as the oldest.

Mom named me for the heroine of that Henry Wadsworth Longfellow poem, written way back in 1847. Mom is generally a pretty smart woman, but she swears it never occurred to her that I might not adore having such a hideous name. Jason's lucky she didn't name *him* Hiawatha.

As for the poem *Evangeline* itself, it's very long and flowery, and a little bit slow to read. I really do like the idea of Evangeline's enduring love for

Gabriel, though. I'd read the whole thing through twice already this summer. Now I looked slowly through the book again, paying particular attention to the black and white drawings. Evangeline didn't seem to bear much resemblance to me. At the very least, I couldn't detect any streaks sprayed in her hair. And she was *always* wearing a dress.

After a while, curiosity began to get the better of me, and I walked over to Griselda's. It was only four blocks away, and there were lots of people watching as I walked. Prestonburg was kind of like Marshfield in that respect. Folks sat on their porches, and kids played on their lawns, and everybody seemed to know what everybody else was doing.

Jason zoomed past on his skateboard when I turned the corner, and a couple of kids watched in near awe as he kickflipped off the sidewalk curbs, sailed up and down the block, spun in fancy turns. He can be an incredible show-off.

Dad and Carolyn were sitting on the front porch. Somebody had managed to open the shutters and windows on the first floor, and the porch looked cleaner. Maybe Miss Lavinia and Miss Estelle had dropped by with a broom. The first thing I checked was the spiderweb over the door. It was gone.

"Vangie!" Dad sounded surprised. He held a glass of something red that looked suspiciously like Cherry Bounce. "Nice of you to join us."

"A pleasure, I'm sure," I told him, trying to

speak in a drawl. It was harder than I realized and came out sounding very peculiar.

"There's a choice of desserts in the kitchen," Carolyn said, "beyond even what Mr. Winthrop led us to believe might be available."

And she was certainly right. I found two pies, the Tuthill sisters' cake, platters of cookies, and a blueberry cobbler. There was ham studded with cloves and pineapple slices in the refrigerator, alongside a couple of Jell-O molds and an open bottle of Cherry Bounce. The windows were open here, too, and a standing fan was pushing the stale air out of the house.

Somebody had tried just about all the desserts. Jason, probably. It was a tough choice, but I finally decided on a thin slice of pecan pie, a bit of blueberry cobbler, and a couple of chocolate chip cookies.

As I headed back to the porch, I could hear Dad and Carolyn talking. I stopped in the front hall and listened, starting in on the cookies.

"What harm could it do just to *list* the house?" Carolyn asked. "Maybe somebody'd buy it right off. It's supposed to be an important local landmark, after all. And then we could get a bigger house back home."

"But this is all so sudden," Dad told her. "And face it, hon, anything we get out of here is found money, whether it's one big chunk or monthly rent. Besides, I kind of *like* the idea of being a southern landowner. And supporting local history."

"What you're supporting," Carolyn reminded him, none too patiently, "is a pair of overly indulged young Californians. It would be nice to have a bit left over for our *own* baby."

Overly indulged, indeed! I waited expectantly for Dad to spring to our defense, but he was strangely silent. Traitor! I stormed back to the kitchen, not even caring if they heard me, and finished the rest of my dessert plate and another big slab of pecan pie. Overly indulged! I was absolutely furious.

But when I went back out front ten minutes later, everybody was all cheery again. I silently seethed through the rest of the evening, till Dad dropped me and Carolyn back at the bed-and-breakfast.

We were sharing a room with twin beds, and Carolyn wanted the lights out. Right away, when I was planning to do my nails over. I'd messed up two of them pretty badly in the course of the day. I was listening to my Walkman and sitting at the little dressing table when she spoke up, from under the covers by the window. Here, at least, there was air-conditioning, a rather noisy window unit.

"How much longer are you going to be up?" Carolyn asked.

I dislodged the Walkman. "Does it matter?"

"I sleep better with the lights out, that's all."

"If you'd let me keep my own room," I pointed out, "my light wouldn't bother you." I wanted to make a crack about being overly indulged, but that would have revealed my eavesdropping too obviously.

She rolled over onto her other side, facing me. "There was no reason to pay for two rooms when we only needed one. Your father's inheritance doesn't change the fact that we aren't rich."

Next thing, she'd be telling me how she grew up poor with holes in her shoes and walked ten miles through the snow in howling blizzards to get to school. I turned off the light, stomped into the bathroom, and finished my nails there. When I came out twenty minutes later, Carolyn was asleep.

I lay awake for a long time, half wishing I'd stayed with Dad and Jason in Griselda's sort-of haunted house, and wondering how they were doing there.

Just dandy, they claimed, when they joined us at eight o'clock in Miss Farnsworth's dining room for breakfast. We were the only guests, but Miss Farnsworth—who trotted back and forth from the kitchen and wore a ruffled, flower-sprigged apron—had laid on tons of food.

"Biscuits, piping hot, fresh out of the oven," Miss Farnsworth announced, setting down a bowl in the middle of the highly polished old table. Fresh flowers in a crystal vase sat beside the sterling salt and pepper shakers. Back home—either of my back-homes, actually—breakfast is a much more casual affair.

"Shouldn't there be bowls for this Cream of

Wheat?" Jason asked, looking into a tureen in front of him.

Carolyn laughed. "That's grits, Jason, and it's not exactly a cereal. It's a southern breakfast food, kind of like . . ."

As she hesitated, Jason put a tiny dollop on his plate and took a tentative nibble. "Wet cement?" he suggested.

"Actually, I was going to say rice, or potatoes. It comes from finely ground hominy, which is a kind of corn." I'm always surprised at the odd bits of information Carolyn comes up with. "And grits is always plural, by the way, but it can take a singular or plural verb."

Dad looked a little glum, and I'd heard him asking Carolyn for some aspirin earlier. "I suppose it's too much to hope that grits is the antidote to Cherry Bounce," he said. He'd had several glasses of the stuff on the front porch of Griselda's last night, and heaven knows how much after we left.

Jason grinned wickedly at him. "You should've just said no, Dad."

We could probably have skipped Miss Farnsworth's breakfast altogether, actually, because when we got to Mr. Winthrop's law office, there was another amazing spread set out on his credenza. There were five different coffee cakes and two kinds of muffins. None of it looked store-bought, either.

The receptionist, Melanie, had another horrible

dress on, this one a pleated shirtwaist in olive green. She was pouring coffee from a silver service into delicate cups when we arrived.

There were a lot of coffee cups and saucers, because a lot of people were there. I counted seven women, most of them on the older side, though I must admit I have trouble figuring out how old adults are. I can tell thirty from seventy, but in between gets kind of fuzzy, particularly in Los Angeles, where so many older women work out all the time and have face lifts and stuff. Nicholas's mother, for instance, looks like she could be his sister. I've heard Mom and Nicholas joking that she has a house charge with the plastic surgeon.

The Tuthill sisters were there, Miss Farnsworth—who must have raced through back yards to beat us, leaping over fences like an Olympic hurdler—and somebody else whose name I couldn't remember, though I'd met her the night before when she brought a plate of divinity, an odd kind of candy. Everybody was excessively friendly, and nobody said a word about my lightning bolt earrings or the turquoise streak in my hair.

They were all looking, though.

Before we got there, the only man in the room had been Mr. Winthrop's grandson, Lee. I just couldn't think of him as a Mr. Anything, even though Dad had warned us that people here were more formal and children weren't supposed to call adults by their first names, the way we do in L.A. Lee was more like an overgrown little kid, and he didn't seem very comfortable being host to this rather formidable group of ladies.

After we got settled in with plates of coffee cake, Mr. Winthrop the Elder (as I'd come to think of him) came in. "Good morning, ladies, Mr. Bradley, Jason. I do apologize for my tardiness, but I was on a long distance telephone call in my grandson's office. Amos Lee," he said to that grandson, who was already cringing, "thank you for helping out here, but I believe you have another engagement?"

It was a dismissal that left no room for argument, and Lee didn't even try to make one. I could tell, though, that he really wished he could stay. I'd have been happy to give him my spot.

Mr. Winthrop the Elder, meanwhile, had ambled over to the credenza and was checking out the coffee cakes. "My gracious, sister Clara," he said, "is this your peach cake?"

The lady who'd been introduced as his sister, Mrs. Clara Clifton, beamed and hustled over to cut him a slice. Then he took a seat behind his desk, and the rest of us settled into chairs around the room. Jason stationed himself directly beside the credenza for easy access to the food.

"Have y'all had an opportunity to introduce yourselves?" he began.

Carolyn smiled graciously. "We met everybody here last night, Mr. Winthrop. Just as you suggested we might."

Mr. Winthrop the Elder grinned. "You give any of them a tour?"

Carolyn shook her head. "We told them you said not to."

"And I don't mind saying some of us found that pretty annoying, Amos," Miss Farnsworth told the lawyer tartly.

"Mildred, he wouldn't let me in, and I'm his own flesh and blood," Mrs. Clifton noted mildly.

Mr. Winthrop the Elder laughed again. "Well, no wonder you ladies are all so twitchety-looking!" He turned to Miss Farnsworth. "Mildred, you want to say anything in particular? Miss Farnsworth is the president of the Kontowoc County Historical Society," he explained to us.

"So we learned this morning," Carolyn said. Dad, in the throes of his Cherry Bounce hangover, seemed quite content to let her do the talking. "It seems we're all pretty much in agreement, Mr. Winthrop. The Historical Society will sign a long-term lease, and we'll leave most of the furnishings intact. Could you draw up a lease for us?"

Mr. Winthrop the Elder pulled out the top drawer of his desk and removed a thin file. "Not wanting to hold up the tour bus this morning, I just happened . . ."

Everybody laughed then except Dad, who gave a slight wince as the noise level rose.

CHAPTER SIX

Things got pretty dull pretty quickly once we returned to Marshfield.

Letters were waiting for me from my friends Stacy and Brianne. Stacy was in France with her whole family, visiting relatives. *Her* parents are still married, which always makes me a little jealous anyway, but to go to *France* seemed exotic beyond belief. She said that her cousins spoke some English and she was trying to learn French, and that Paris was extremely sophisticated.

Stacy's letter made me homesick, even though she wasn't at home at all. In fact, most of my friends weren't in L.A. this summer. Lauren was going to two sessions of volleyball camp, and Jennifer was staying with her father—her *real* father, not one of the steps—in Portland. Only Brianne was at home, and her letter said she was really bored. If I were home, I thought wistfully, we could at least be bored together.

Dad rented a video of *Gone with the Wind*, which I'd never seen before. After our experiences in the Deep South, I found it fascinating. I watched it three times, wondering what on earth was wrong with Scarlett O'Hara. How could she pine over that wishy-washy Ashley Wilkes when Rhett Butler wanted her? The lady was nuts!

Dad was working his usual long hours, and Carolyn was at her shop every day. I'd worried about what I would find to do this summer and had brought along a stack of books and a small bead-work loom, with four or five million beads in every imaginable color. I was intending to make friendship bracelets for my friends at home, but I'd gotten sidetracked on a few sets of earrings. The ones for Mom's birthday in September were already done, and I'd finished one of a pair for myself, an inch wide and nearly three inches long, an original design made of all sparkly beads.

But I was bored, too, so much so that I'd actually taken to walking down to Carolyn's Gift Exchange some afternoons just to hang out.

It's a bizarre kind of store, specializing in brand-new gifts that people want to exchange for something else but can't take back to the original store for one reason or another. There are tables full of hot doggers and garlic bakers and late-night-TV steak knives and cookie jars shaped like skunks and pineapples. Deviled egg plates and aprons that say KISS THE COOK, STUPID and jillions of ice buckets, each more atrocious than the last. One wall is covered with trivets and inspirational plaques and awful wall clocks.

She has signs around saying things like YOUR I-HATE-IT IS SOMEBODY ELSE'S GOTTA-HAVE and ONE PERSON'S WHITE ELEPHANT IS ANOTHER'S CHERISHED TREASURE. People get a credit for whatever they bring in. The catch is, they have to spend it on other junk from the store.

Two weeks after we got back, the stuff from Prestonburg was delivered. Dad and Carolyn had gone through Miss Griselda's house pretty thoroughly, including an attic that we discovered after taking the Historical Society ladies through on tour. They'd boxed up odd lamps and candlesticks and end tables and knickknacks and some of the more interesting rocks. They'd also arranged to ship home Philip Patterson's big rolltop desk, which stood now in the middle of the living room, looking very old. It also looked enormous, even bigger than it had seemed in Mississippi.

Carolyn had insisted on waiting till Dad got home from work to go through anything, so we'd wolfed down dinner the moment he walked through the door. Grandpa was over, too, going through the booty with us. Carolyn had just finished rubbing an almond stick into a couple of little scratches on the desk and was carefully rolling open the front of it. All the pigeonholes were empty now, of course, but I was surprised at just how many little doors and nooks and crannies there were.

"Don't these old desks usually have secret compartments?" Carolyn asked.

Dad reached past her and pulled out an upright drawer beside the center inside door. It was carved like some kind of ornate pillar. And it was empty.

"That's pretty obvious, isn't it?" Carolyn asked.

"Let me look," Jason offered eagerly, and began poking and probing all around the desk's innards. A bit roughly, it seemed to me.

Grandpa seemed to agree. "Easy does it," he counseled, moving in closer. "Try this. Open that little door and then press on the back wall behind it."

Jason opened the door and pushed on the back. Nothing happened, and he pushed harder.

"Careful!" Carolyn warned sharply.

"You shouldn't need to use force," Grandpa said mildly. "Try pressing on the very bottom part."

Jason tried again . . . and this time a little compartment opened in the back!

"Wow!" he yelped. "There's a secret compartment here!" He thrust his fingers inside. "But it's empty," he said a moment later, trying to hide his disappointment.

We all crowded around to look at what he'd found. Grandpa looked pensive for a moment. Then he examined the inner reaches of the desk, tentatively poking and prodding. After several failed attempts, he suddenly said, "Hey!"

A little panel opened in the back wall of the desk. There were papers inside it.

"There's something in there, Grandpa!" Jason

chirped. His voice is starting to change, but when he gets excited, it gets real high and embarrasses him.

Grandpa very carefully removed two envelopes. One was yellowed with age and addressed:

TO BE OPENED UPON MY DEATH BY THE SURVIVING MALE DESCENDANTS OF LANGLEY PATTERSON, ESQUIRE

The other envelope was newer and addressed, in a funny handwriting, with flourishes, to Ronald Bradley. Dad.

Grandpa handed both envelopes to Dad. "Your mail, Son."

Dad shook his head in wonder. He opened the letter addressed to him and read out loud:

"My dear great-nephew,
 Someday you may find this letter from my grandfather, Langley Patterson. I discovered this secret drawer by accident after my dear father went to his eternal reward. It belongs to you as the closest living male relative.
                              Fondly,
                              Griselda Patterson
May 14, 1960"

Dad looked up at us with a stunned expression. "This is very weird," I noted. Nobody else said anything.

Then Dad opened the other letter, very, very carefully. A small old-fashioned key fell out, and Jason grabbed it from the floor. Dad pulled out some folded sheets of paper, looked at them a moment, then yawned nonchalantly. "I've got an early meeting tomorrow . . ."

"Dad!" Jason howled.

Dad smiled and looked around at us. "Vangie's right," he said. "This is very weird indeed. Brace yourselves, gang. This letter appears to be a poem." He read:

> *"Oh, knowledge is a fleeting thing*
> *   Possessing Such makes one a king.*
> *When man has ended worldly strife*
> *   Oh, still goes on most glorious life."*

It sounded like a colossal joke. Carolyn gently took the letter from Dad and sank into a chair beside the rolltop desk. The desk looked like it was grinning at us. Carolyn seemed suddenly consumed by weariness. She continued reading aloud:

> *"When Heavenbound our spirits climb*
> *   Our earthly wealth is left behind.*
> *But have ye knowledge, heir of mine,*
> *   You shall my hidden treasure find."*

She stopped abruptly.

"Hidden treasure!" Jason's voice rose a full octave. "Where's the map?"

Carolyn looked through the other pages. Slowly. Deliberately. She can be really infuriating. "There isn't one. Just a lot more poetry, and I use the term very loosely. It seems to be . . . a test."

"You mean like school?" I asked, confused.

"Sort of," Carolyn answered. "There are a lot of individual clues. It looks like a test of general knowledge. The idea is to solve each of the various clues and then take letters from the answers to find where the treasure is."

"There a date on that letter?" Grandpa wanted to know.

"March 5, 1883," Carolyn told him, glancing at the first page.

"Not to burst anybody's bubble," Grandpa said, "but that's more than a hundred years ago. Maybe there was a treasure once, but it doesn't seem very likely it'd still be there. Somebody might well have found it. Or there's also the possibility that somebody put a big old shopping mall over it."

I looked at him. "There's no such thing as a shopping mall in Prestonburg, Grandpa. There's barely any shopping at all." Downtown Prestonburg consisted of a couple of smallish stores and two churches. Plus, now, a Historical Society building. I had a vision of all those Historical Society ladies working feverishly on Miss Griselda's house, wearing flower-sprigged aprons and rubber gloves and singing "Whistle While You Work" like the Seven Dwarfs.

Jason cocked his head. "I, uh, wasn't always paying total attention when old Mr. Winthrop was talking. Did he say anything about a treasure, Dad? Or about a treasure being found?"

"Not to me," Dad replied. He'd suddenly gotten very serious. Maybe he was picturing a chest full of Confederate gold.

"Then, who knows?" Jason said cheerfully. "It could still be there. It could *easily* still be there. And I'm gonna try to find it," he added with sudden resolution.

"How?" I asked. Not to burst anybody's bubble.

Grandpa took the letter from Carolyn and looked through it thoughtfully. "Well," he suggested, "there's always the library."

But Jason was looking beyond that. "When we find the treasure," he announced, "I'm gonna get half a dozen custom-made skateboards and a TV as big as that wall." He smirked at me. "I'll keep it in my own room, with a lock on the door."

"How typically generous," I told him. "*I'll* get a red convertible."

"With a chauffeur?" Grandpa asked. "Or did I miss when they lowered the age for a driver's license?"

"I'll get a handsome young out-of-work actor for my chauffeur," I decided on the spot, thinking of Larry Turner and "Wellington's World." It was too grim to think about how long it would be before I got my own license. "And then when he becomes famous—"

"—he'll hate you because you remind him of his past," Jason said. I was surprised he could be so perceptive. Maybe he'd talked to Larry Turner about more than those dogs. "What'll you do, Dad?"

"Hmmm," he said thoughtfully. "I guess the first order of business would be a great big four-bedroom house, so you guys could have your own rooms when you visit."

I gave him a big hug. "That *would* be nice," I agreed, with a smug glance at Carolyn. Though she'd probably just have a bunch more babies to fill those bedrooms up right away.

"And then," Dad went on, "after I'd put away enough to cover your college tuitions, I'd kind of like to get a big four-wheel-drive van, to get to the cottage I'd build up in the North Woods. How about you, Carolyn? What would you like?"

No stepchildren, I thought, though I didn't dare say it.

"I'd like to hire an assistant in the shop," she replied, sounding very tired. "And get a cook and a cleaning lady. Maybe some stock in the power company, too, 'cause it'll cost a fortune to heat that big house you want." She thought a moment and smiled. "And if there's anything left over, I'd like a baby grand piano."

"I didn't realize you played," Grandpa told her. Neither did I, though I was fairly sure there was plenty I didn't know about Carolyn. Or want to know, to be perfectly honest.

"I don't," she admitted. "But I've always wanted to learn. And now, unless there's more hypothetical fortune to spend, I'm going to bed. I'm *totally* exhausted."

After Grandpa left and everybody went to bed, I found I couldn't sleep. I'd been kind of uncomfortable in the guest bedroom anyway, ever since the day we arrived when I started to unpack. The closet and drawers were jammed with all sorts of baby clothing and paraphernalia, stuff Carolyn had picked up as it came available at the Gift Exchange.

So I knew that this was the last time the room would be mine, and somehow it wasn't as friendly anymore. It didn't even feel much like the refuge I'd always considered it. In previous years, the room had been my sanctuary when I got bored or depressed or homesick or just tired of hearing Carolyn talk about how much things cost.

It was a small, cozy room, with the eaves coming down on one side. There's an old quilt in the double wedding ring pattern made by Carolyn's great-grandmother on the bed, and an antique dresser with fancy brass drawer pulls. A little desk sits in the alcove by the window, and when you sit at the desk, you can look out at the yard below.

But this was the baby's room now. The next time I came here there'd be a crib set up, and a changing table with a Disney musical mobile over it. The mobile was already in the closet, just waiting for me to leave.

The funny thing was, I was really kind of excited about the baby, and secretly hoping it would be a girl. A little sister, even a long-distance half sister, would be nice. I haven't spent much time around little kids, other than Jason and his buddies, and I don't like baby-sitting very much. But somehow this felt different.

I sat down at the little desk and looked out the window for a while. Tonight there was a big old full moon. And down in the yard, fireflies blinked on and off. I adore fireflies. They're so romantic and mysterious. They may be my favorite thing about Minnesota. Other than Dad and Grandpa, of course.

I wasn't really sleepy at all, so I went downstairs quietly. I found the letter from Langley Patterson inside the rolltop desk and sat down to read it all the way through.

TO BE OPENED UPON MY DEATH BY THE SURVIVING MALE DESCENDANTS OF LANGLEY PATTERSON, ESQUIRE

Oh, knowledge is a fleeting thing
  Possessing Such makes one a king.
When man has ended worldly strife
  Oh, still goes on most glorious life.

When Heavenbound our spirits climb
     Our earthly wealth is left behind.
But have ye knowledge, heir of mine,
     You shall my hidden treasure find.

The Labyrinth of my design
     Became my son's prison, and mine.
Away we flew, his wings did melt
     My name's fourth letter will you help.

She headed west, with lover bold
     In search of California gold.
Her journey's tale a song became
     Third letter of that lady's name?

A lady rising from a shell
     Has made the world my praises tell.
Florentine art owed much to me
     My name's fifth letter will help thee.

My properties make special food
     From something which itself is good.
A young one dies and that is how
     My third will help your progress now.

The man who built the cotton gin
     Did help the South its fortune win.
But 'twas the North from whence he came
     Second letter of his home state's name?

When no white man lived in this county
     A settler came to seek his bounty.

Plantation owner he became
  First letter of his wife's first name?

No polecat I, I tried to be
  An honor to Commander Lee
Abroad returned from whence I came
  Last letter of my final name?

One moon has earth, a sight of glory
  Bold Jupiter's a different story
Its moons shine bright while here we slumber
  The second when you write their number?

The Carolina Parrot flies
  Aloft in Mississippi skies
The color of his head is true
  Its final letter one more clue.

I start as pink, but change my hue
  To purple as my life is through
Then pink once more, a final time
  My second letter place in line.

Twelve brothers we in ancient day
  And one of us was sold away
One of our names had seven letters
  Its fourth will make your fortune better.

Though Vivarini painted here
  My fame results from something clear.
Drop it down and it will shatter.
  My first letter is the one to matter.

A grievous error made I when
  Cordelia's love I failed to ken.

71

The bard preserved my tragic tale.
  Take my third and you won't fail.

You've solved these puzzles, knowledged one?
  Your work is very nearly done.
Now take these letters you have found
  And move them carefully around.
A name they'll make in proper order
  A site within the County border.
There stand and look round thoroughly
  And find two giant live oak trees.
Walk 'tween them then, your paces measure.
  At 118 there lies the treasure.
There find a small and hidden hole
  When you away a large stone roll.
Your knowledge served you well, my son—
  Your days of wealth have now begun!

I read the whole thing twice. Clearly it was ridiculous, and the references to "male descendant" and "son" really annoyed me. And yet . . . maybe the idea of trying to solve it wasn't so crazy after all. It certainly couldn't *hurt* to spend a little time at the library. We weren't exactly overscheduled these days.

All right, it was a long shot, but miracles happen, every single day.

And if we *did* come up with anything, surely Dad would share it with us. He hadn't cut us off, after all, when we were making all those silly plans for spending the treasure. The whole thing was based on the notion of ancestors and descendants. Jason and I were Dad's descendants, the only ones until the baby was born.

And, hey, I'm generous enough. Bring on the baby. I could stand making a three-way split of the lost Confederate gold.

CHAPTER
SEVEN

Where to begin?

That was the question we tackled the next morning at breakfast with Grandpa. He came over bright and early at eight-thirty, carrying an apple-raisin coffee cake from his favorite Swedish bakery, which was every bit as good as what the Historical Society ladies in Prestonburg had plied us with. Jason had been up since dawn, executing spins on the skateboard ramp, but I didn't stir till I heard the doorbell ring.

When I'd gotten dressed and was half-awake, we powwowed at the kitchen table. In the light of day, a big part of me thought the whole thing was a ridiculous waste of time. But I have to admit that another part of me considered Langley Patterson's treasure hunt a genuine adventure.

With the possibility of considerable rewards.

"It's been my experience," Grandpa began, "that when I'm faced with some kind of overwhelming chore, I need to break it down. Then I start out with the least onerous task and work my way up."

"What's 'onerous'?" Jason asked.

"Awful," I told him. "Burdensome, hideous, oppressive, arduous, difficult." Nicely timed, Grandpa. *Onerous* had been a Word of Power in English class right before school got out.

"What's 'arduous'?" Jason asked.

"Onerous," I told him irritably. "So what you're saying, then, is we should take the easy clues first?"

Grandpa smiled. "Exactly. Now, I stopped by right before your dad went to work and picked up Langley Patterson's letter. These are photocopies, one set for each of us to work from. The original is probably safest if we leave it in the desk. I suggest that we adjourn from here to the Marshfield Public Library and just plow into it."

Which is pretty much what we did.

The Marshfield Public Library was built by the Carnegie Foundation in 1912. It's a two-story red brick building on Central Avenue in downtown Marshfield. Back when the library was built, it was the largest for twenty miles. Now, as Minneapolis has grown out into the surrounding countryside, Marshfield is a suburb that connects with other suburbs in every direction. The library, however, is still one of the best around, according to Grandpa Bradley.

It was another hot, sticky morning, though certainly not as miserable as Mississippi. I'd gained a new appreciation for Minnesota weather after my sojourn in the south. The warm season might be short, but it didn't totally annihilate you. The library had big fans in the tall, double-hung windows, and it really wasn't too uncomfortable inside.

Jason teamed up with Grandpa, and I worked on my own. A couple of the clues seemed pretty easy, but Grandpa had assigned those to Jason and himself at breakfast. He'd given me a little wink so I'd realize he was trying to encourage Jason.

Not a bad idea, actually. Jason is what my therapist stepfather Nicholas calls an academically unmotivated student and I call just plain lazy. Ever since kindergarten, he's been a classroom cutup who always just manages to slip under the wire with his assignments. That's part of what makes him fun to be around and, I suspect, fun to be with in class. It also means he never cracks a book unless he has to. So far this summer, the only thing I'd seen him reading was his skateboarding magazines, which Mom was conscientiously forwarding. And those are mostly pictures.

I parked myself between the forty-pound dictionary and a set of encyclopedias and began. There were thirteen clues altogether, and Grandpa had assigned the first eight to himself and Jason. That left me five, all to myself. At breakfast it had seemed manageable enough, but suddenly I felt overwhelmed, and not a little silly.

Least onerous first, I reminded myself.

So I started at the bottom:

A grievous error made I when
    Cordelia's love I failed to ken.
The bard preserved my tragic tale.
    Take my third and you won't fail.

My mother is a high school English teacher, so of course I knew that the Bard meant Shakespeare. I found a volume of *Complete Works of Shakespeare* on the shelf, but it was discouragingly fat. Thirty-seven plays he'd written, and more than a hundred and fifty sonnets. Where to begin? I started flipping idly through the thick volume, which featured double columns of very small type. Then I checked the table of contents. The name Cordelia didn't appear in the titles of any plays or poems.

All right, I decided, I'll just start with the more famous plays. Or at least the ones I'd already heard of. I'd never actually *read* any of them. I looked through *Romeo and Juliet, Hamlet, Othello.* No Cordelia anywhere, though I did keep running across expressions I'd heard without knowing their origin. Somebody had made a lot of pencil marks in the margins beside famous quotes. I know you're not supposed to mark up library books, but to be perfectly honest, I was glad they had. Lots of things were marked, and many of them I'd actually heard.

"To be, or not to be: that is the question" was marked in *Hamlet.* As was "O! that this too too solid flesh would melt." I laughed out loud when I found that one. It's what Mom always says when she's dieting.

I found "the ides of March" in *Julius Caesar* and "Double, double toil and trouble; Fire burn, and cauldron bubble" in *Macbeth*. It was really amazing to think that one person had written so many memorable lines, things that we were still quoting all over the place four hundred years later. Had Shakespeare realized, I wondered, that this might happen? Would he have written any differently if he'd known?

But I wasn't finding my answer, and the more I got sidetracked checking out the pencil-marked passages, the less actual progress I made. I looked across the room. Jason and Grandpa were hunched over a table, plotting feverishly.

Then, purely by accident, I stumbled on *King Lear.* Cordelia was there! I went through enough of it to figure out that King Lear was her father, and the unappreciative parent. So I had an answer, finally: LEAR. The third letter was *A*, which didn't exactly lead to a revelation about what the other twelve letters might be.

Then I had a funny feeling. On a hunch, I looked up Cordelia in the dictionary, and there she was, identified as King Lear's daughter. I could have saved myself a lot of time, I realized in annoyance, if I'd checked there first.

Though I didn't really regret, when I thought about it, seeing where all those famous quotes had come from.

I turned to the next clue:

Though Vivarini painted here
 My fame results from something clear.
Drop it down and it will shatter.
 My first letter is the one to matter.

This time I started in the dictionary, which didn't even mention Vivarini. Back to the encyclopedia, where there turned out to be several of them. The Vivarinis were Italian painters of altarpieces and other religious art in the fifteenth century. But I wasn't really interested in the particulars of their careers, just in where they'd painted. They lived in Venice, famous for its canals and gondolas, on the island of Murano. By backtracking to the *I* volume and Italy, I discovered that Murano has been a famous glassmaking center practically forever.

So MURANO was my answer, and its first letter *M*.

A-M? M-A? Clearly I'd need more.

But I was on a roll, feeling supercharged and pretty clever as I looked through my three remaining verses and selected the next one to tackle:

The Carolina Parrot flies
 Aloft in Mississippi skies
The color of his head is true
 Its final letter one more clue.

That sounded straightforward enough, even easy. But I ran into an unexpected problem: The Carolina parrot (also known as the Carolina parakeet) was extinct, and had been since the early twentieth century. The encyclopedia told me its Latin name was *Conuropsis carolinensis* and that it had sometimes gone as far north as Ontario. But no picture.

I felt really stumped, and a little annoyed. Obviously Langley Patterson hadn't thought about extinction—except maybe his own—when he wrote this test. What had happened to the Carolina parrot, anyway? Parrots are pretty birds, after all, worth a lot of money if you want to buy one and have it sit in your kitchen window. Our next-door neighbor in L.A. has a huge blue macaw that cost thousands of dollars.

Maybe the birds were extinct because they'd been collected from the wild for pets. *That* was a depressing thought.

When I finally admitted to myself that I wasn't going to get any further without help, I went to the reference librarian and told her what I was trying to find out. "It's a test of general knowledge," I explained, not wanting to get into my loony ancestors and their weird habits.

The librarian was a peppy little woman with very curly hair and an infectious smile. She thought for a moment, then raised one finger and widened the smile. "Audubon!" she announced, and marched off into the stacks.

I followed her to the 500s, where she pulled a

large book off the shelf. She frowned slightly and blew dust off its top before opening it.

The Birds of America, it was called, by John James Audubon. She checked the index, then flipped triumphantly to what was identified as the Carolina paroquet. The picture was a cheerful one, a flock of bright green birds squawking in some branches. Their faces were a kind of orangey-brown, but the rest of their heads were a vibrant, defiant yellow.

Bingo! Langley had asked for the last letter of YELLOW. With the new *W*, I could rearrange my letters, but they still didn't come out to much. L-A-W. A-W-L. W-A-L. A-L-W. L-W-A. W-L-A. Not much to go on.

I carried the Audubon book back to the table where I'd been working and looked through it. I'd heard of the Audubon Society, but I'd never known anything about the man it was named for, and he turned out to be a pretty interesting guy. A Frenchman who came to America at seventeen, he spent years painting birds in their natural habitats. It seems like an obvious enough idea, but nobody had done that before.

The pictures were kind of stylized, but amazingly detailed. The book's introduction mentioned some other extinct birds, and I looked them up, too. The great auk was two feet long, cumbersome-looking and flightless, with interesting little stripes on its bill. I was surprised to find out that the last time anybody'd seen a great auk was 1844, nearly forty years before Langley had written his test. So there *had* been extinct birds already, then. I wondered if anybody had much noticed, or cared.

The extinct Labrador duck just looked like a duck to me, but the passenger pigeon was more interesting, soft gray with a rosy breast. Curious, I went back to the reference librarian, who helped me find a book with more about these extinct birds.

Talk about depressing!

The great auk had been hunted to extinction when museum directors realized only about fifty were left alive and that there were only a couple of stuffed ones in museums. The birds were living on a remote island off Iceland, where they'd swum after surviving a volcanic eruption. But just when they were probably congratulating themselves on their narrow escape, hunters tracked them down and killed every last one. So they could be stuffed for *museums.*

The passenger pigeon story was even worse. There'd once been *billions* of them, darkening the skies as they flew overhead, in flocks of millions, for days on end. They made good eating, kind of like chicken, and had kept the Pilgrims alive in the harsh winter of 1648.

I wondered what went through the minds of the people who hunted them down. There were a lot of nasty massacre techniques, but the absolute worst, I thought, was capturing a live pigeon, sewing its eyes shut, and then setting it on a stool, or perch.

When it cried out for help, these original "stool pigeons" inadvertently set up their buddies to be shot. Whole flocks at a time.

And as for the Carolina parakeets, they weren't eaten, or put in cages, or even collected much for museums. They were just shot 'cause folks thought they were pests.

You can imagine how depressed I was when Jason and Grandpa appeared beside me.

"Lunch, anybody?" Grandpa asked. "I'd suggest getting some food and then reporting on our morning's progress. Jason here claims to be weak from hunger."

Weak Jason maintained that only cheeseburgers would satisfy his burning hunger, a claim made partly to torture his vegetarian sister, I know. At least he hadn't asked for chicken. We went to a fast food joint not far from the library, a place that also offered a pretty uninspired salad.

"So," Grandpa said, when we were all seated and Jason was chomping into the first of the three burgers he'd ordered. "How went the morning's research, Vangie?"

"I'm three for three," I told them proudly, my depression over the extinct birds momentarily set aside. This wasn't so terribly hard after all, I'd decided. Though I'd just looked at my two remaining clues. One was frighteningly vague, and the other an unnervingly specific reference to ancient history, a subject about which I know less than nothing.

"Beat you," Jason announced. With his mouth full, the little heathen. "We got four."

"Don't look so crushed, Vangie," Grandpa told me, with a pat on the shoulder. "Two of them were quite easy, and I knew the general direction to head for the others." He put some catsup on his french fries. "Now, let's share what we've got so far. Which is, let's not forget, more than half of the puzzle."

I told them the answers I'd found then, and they gave me theirs. We were all feeling pretty smug, clear through soft ice cream cones for dessert, until it was actually time to go back to the library. I wasn't the only one who was hesitant, it turned out.

"I don't mind saying," Grandpa remarked, as we got into his car, "that I'm a little concerned about what we'll be able to come up with this afternoon." I'd waited out of habit for him to unlock the doors, completely forgetting that in Marshfield nobody ever bothered locking their cars. "The flaw in my least-onerous-first theory is that eventually you get left with all the hard stuff."

Which turned out to be quite true.

Grandpa had suggested I try the book of Genesis in the Old Testament of the Bible for my ancient history clue:

Twelve brothers we in ancient day
And one of us was sold away

One of our names had seven letters
    Its fourth will make your fortune better.

I had the King James Version of the Bible, which didn't exactly make for easy reading. We go to a Unitarian church in L.A., and there's not much talk about the Old Testament. I read through chapter after chapter of lists of names, men said to have lived hundreds of years, women who bore endless children. I was getting pretty bleary by the time I reached Chapter 37, and found Joseph sold into slavery for twenty pieces of silver by his brothers.

Bingo!

Finding the names of those brothers was another matter, though, and the idea of going *back* through all those lists of names didn't excite me much. Finally, it occurred to me to check the encyclopedia, and there they were listed, the twelve sons of Jacob who came to head the Twelve Tribes of Israel: Reuben, Simeon, Levi, Judah, Issachar, Zebulon, Joseph, Benjamin, Dan, Naphtali, Gad, and Asher.

The one whose name had seven letters was ZEBULON, which gave us a *U*.

But then I was stuck. I spent another hour or so on my last clue:

I start as pink, but change my hue
    To purple as my life is through
Then pink once more, a final time
    My second letter place in line.

I tried clouds, which didn't work at all, and flowers, which offered a zillion possibilities. I thought about baby animals, starting out pink and aging, but then the business about getting pink again really threw me.

Maybe it was a method of paint preparation, but that didn't seem to me to be very fair. It also involved a lot of complicated chemistry that I couldn't imagine Langley being familiar with.

Feathers? Vegetables as they cook? Some offbeat reference to sunrise and daytime and sunset?

I was stumped. And it didn't even make me feel a lot better when we all got together and I learned that Jason and Grandpa hadn't solved *any* clues that afternoon. Jason and I were both pretty bummed out.

"Hey," Grandpa said, putting two fingers under my chin and lifting it. "Let's get this in perspective, gang. We took a century-old general knowledge test, and in a matter of hours in a modern public library, we came up with eight out of thirteen answers." He grinned. "I don't know about you kids, but I'm feeling pretty smart, myself."

CHAPTER EIGHT

That night in the living room we set up a dry erase board Dad had brought home from work and our information from the library. We deliberately hadn't told Dad and Carolyn anything about our results, making a big production out of teasing them.

Now, finally, it was time.

"Jason will begin our report," Grandpa announced. "And I think it's safe to say that our time today was spent very profitably. If you catch my drift."

Carolyn perked right up, I noticed. I thought I saw the faint flicker of dollar signs in her eyes.

"Now, let me see if I've got this straight," she said. "There are thirteen clues and after you solve each one you take a specific letter from the answer." She must have been the kind of student who always sat in the front row and raised her hand constantly in class. "Just please don't take it personally, kids, if I nod off in the middle of the presentation," she said, yawning.

"Seems to me you're working too hard," Grandpa told her, looking worried.

"Not really," she answered. "My doctor says it's common to be this tired when you're pregnant. Particularly when you've waited awhile to have your first baby."

Her *first* baby? So she *was* planning to make this a habit!

"I'll try to keep it lively," Jason promised. He consulted the legal pad he was holding. "The first clue that Grandpa and I solved was this one:

The man who built the cotton gin
*   Did help the South its fortune win.*
But 'twas the North from whence he came
*   Second letter of his home state's name?*

Now, Eli Whitney invented the cotton gin." He spoke with familiarity, but I had a feeling that was something he'd just learned that morning. "And he was born in Massachusetts. That gives us an *A*."

Jason wrote MASSACHUSETTS on the dry erase board and neatly circled the first *A*. "Our next one was this:

A lady rising from a shell
*   Has made the world my praises tell.*
Florentine art owed much to me
*   My name's fifth letter will help thee.*

Carolyn, Grandpa says you'd know that without looking it up."

Carolyn's smile was a little smug. "Well, I *did* major in art history in college." The perfect background for running a junk shop. "And that would have to be Botticelli. *The Birth of Venus*. Though we always called it *Venus on the Half Shell*."

At this, Jason triumphantly produced a color plate of the painting. Ever since he'd realized it featured a naked lady, he'd been behaving like the little kid he really still is.

It was a striking enough picture, though. Venus had a lot of long blond hair, though not quite enough to get her properly covered. A pair of wind gods on one side were blowing, as if to cool her off (rather unnecessary, under the circumstances) and a woman on the other side was racing over with some kind of cloak. I made an effort to act unembarrassed, but I really didn't see the need for Jason to leave the book sitting open to that page as he continued.

"The fifth letter of BOTTICELLI," he announced as he wrote it on the board and made the appropriate circle, "is *I*. And the next one was actually pretty easy:

One moon has earth, a sight of glory
Bold Jupiter's a different story
Its moons shine bright while here we slumber
The second when you write their number?

Jupiter has twelve moons, and the second letter in TWELVE is *W*." He added the information.

"The last one that Jason and I found today comes from mythology," Grandpa announced.

Jason picked up the paper, quickly glanced again at Venus's picture, then read:

> *"The Labyrinth of my design*
> > *Became my son's prison, and mine.*
> *Away we flew, his wings did melt*
> > *My name's fourth letter will you help."*

"You know," Dad said slowly, "that actually sounds familiar. Wasn't it Ichabod or Icarus or something like that?"

Carolyn perked up. "No, Icarus was the son, Ron. The one whose wax wings melted when he got too close to the sun. But I can't remember the father's name."

Grandpa shook his head with mock sadness. "The father always gets forgotten. He was Daedalus."

Jason wrote DAEDALUS on the board and circled the second *D*.

"An interesting fellow, Daedalus," Grandpa continued. "He was quite an inventor, though most of what he invented seems to have been done to get himself out of some mess that inventing something else had caused."

I was getting lost here. "What do you mean, Grandpa?"

He considered for a moment. "Well, all of this took place on the island of Crete under King Minos. Daedalus had been indirectly involved in the unfortunate creation of a loathsome creature that was half man and half bull. The Minotaur, it was called. So then he had to invent a place to keep it, and he came up with the first labyrinth, or maze. Every ninth year they'd throw in seven young Athenian maidens and men as sacrifices to the Minotaur."

"How disgusting," I muttered.

"Can't argue that one, Vangie," Grandpa acknowledged. "But finally, the third time the young people were supposed to be sacrificed, a young fellow named Theseus went in to slay the Minotaur. The problem had always been that Daedalus did too good a job designing the Labyrinth. Nobody could ever find their way out. A young woman named Ariadne gave Theseus a ball of thread to unravel as he went in, so that after he slew the Minotaur—which he did, by the way, and very nicely—he could get back out."

Grandpa sighed. "By now Daedalus had decided that maybe he didn't want to be involved with King Minos anymore, but the king had other ideas. He shut up Daedalus and his son, Icarus, in the Labyrinth. But Daedalus, being an inventor, figured if they couldn't get out on ground level, maybe they could fly. It's one of the first recorded instances of man and aviation, and only marginally successful. Daedalus made them a couple of pairs of wax and feather wings. Icarus, who like most young men didn't pay enough attention to what his father told him, flew too close to the sun and his wings melted."

"Did Langley Patterson really know all this stuff?" I wondered aloud. The subject had been on my mind all day. For one thing, Langley didn't have access to the Marshfield Public Library. Or, quite possibly, *any* library, other than whatever books they'd had at the Wishing Rock Plantation.

"The concept of an educated man has eroded somewhat over the years, I'm sorry to say," Grandpa answered slowly. "Yes, Langley probably did know all of this, and a good deal more. We're lucky he didn't write the whole thing in Latin, for that matter. Back then, a knowledge of Latin and Greek was considered an essential part of being an educated man." He looked at me and held a hand up. "And before you start complaining, Vangie, it wasn't *my* fault that women didn't get the same education men did."

Grandpa grinned. "On the other hand, Langley Patterson would undoubtedly have trouble operating a computer. Or even an ATM machine." He stood and stretched. "Vangie, it's time for your part of the program."

I crossed over a little self-consciously to the dry erase board. Carolyn was definitely nodding off, and Dad had mentioned something earlier about maybe needing to go to the hospital. So I made my part brief.

When I was finished, Carolyn was sound asleep on the couch, and the dry erase board looked like this:

M **A** SSACHUSETTS
BOTT **I** CELLI
T **W** ELVE
DAE **D** ALUS
YELLO **W**
ZEB **U** LON
M URANO
LE **A** R
A I W D W U M A

"So the treasure's at Aiwdwuma, is it?" Dad gave a little chuckle.

"Actually, we've got a few more to solve," Jason admitted.

"Actually, we're stumped," Grandpa said. "But only for the moment. There are five clues left, and one of them is almost impossible, at least from here. It calls for the name of the wife of the first white man who settled in Kontowoc County, Mississippi. Not surprisingly, that information just isn't available in Marshfield, Minnesota."

"Couldn't you just write to the Historical Society and ask?" Dad suggested.

Jason looked horrified. "That'd tip them off!"

"To what?" Dad asked.

"That we're looking for the treasure!" Jason answered.

Grandpa nodded. "It's entirely possible that Langley Patterson's treasure is a local legend. For all we know, folks have been searching for it for generations, and they might have purposely kept it secret from you."

"I can't really imagine keeping *anything* secret for more than five minutes in Prestonburg," Dad told him. "But maybe you've got a point. What about those other clues, though?"

"The others will simply take more time," Grandpa answered soothingly. "But I have every confidence in the troops here."

Everyone was quiet for a moment.

"The thing is," I said slowly, "what happens when we do solve it?"

Dad frowned. "What do you mean?" He can be *so* deliberately dense.

"I mean," I told him, "that once we've solved all thirteen clues, we have to go to Mississippi to find the actual treasure. There's not much point in doing all this work if we can't benefit from it."

Dad looked uncomfortable. I don't think it had occurred to him before that we might actually be able to do it. "This whole thing is awfully iffy, Vangie. Starting with *if* there ever was a treasure in the first place. The Patterson family is beyond idiosyncrasy, moving into the realm of just plain nuts. There's a good chance that this entire business was just a big old joke."

"There's also a chance it was a big old treasure," Jason pointed out, looking worried.

"So, all right," Dad went on. "Say there actually *was* a treasure. If it's still there a hundred years later, it's probably because it was hidden extremely well. Maybe so well that nobody will ever find it, even after solving Langley Patterson's puzzle."

"If it's that well hidden," I argued, "it's because you can *only* find it by solving the puzzle. Think about it, Dad. When Langley did this, he had no way of knowing how quickly his puzzle would be found. Apparently his son Philip never found it at all. And Griselda was too cowed by the sexism of the letter, all the stuff about first *son*, to even consider doing it herself."

"So?" Dad asked.

"So he'd have built that uncertainty into his plan. The guy was well educated, and smart enough to devise this kind of puzzle. He'd allow for the fact that he didn't know how soon somebody'd go looking. He'd choose a place that was likely to remain unchanged."

Dad looked thoughtful. "Tell you what," he said finally. "If you can actually solve the rest of the clues, all but that one about the wife of the first settler in the county, then yes, we'll go back." I glanced at Carolyn, who was still sound asleep. Just as well. I suspected she'd make a real fuss about this offer once she learned about it.

Jason jumped across the room and almost knocked Dad over. I got up with a lot more restraint and offered my own hug. Over Dad's shoulder, Grandpa gave me a big wink.

When the hug was over, Dad smiled fondly at us both. "Just one little thing, though."

"What?" I asked warily. Whenever adults say "just one little thing," it's usually monumental. And onerous.

He pointed to the third word on our list, TWELVE.

"I'd think about this one a little," he said. "The twelve moons of Jupiter."

"What about them?" Jason asked. "I looked it up in an astronomy book."

"Precisely," Dad answered. "And I bet it was a relatively current astronomy book. But a hundred years ago, an astronomy book would probably have given a smaller number of moons. Telescopes weren't as strong back then. You know, the planet Pluto wasn't even discovered until the twentieth century. They could easily have missed some itty-bitty moons."

"Not half-bad," Jason told him admiringly.

Dad beamed. We had him hooked, I could tell.

CHAPTER NINE

The next morning, I was prepared to sleep until noon.

Jason had other ideas. Around nine he started making a lot of noise right outside my bedroom door. By the time he actually stuck his head in and asked if I was awake, I was ready to strangle him, but I certainly wasn't going to be able to get back to sleep. So I grabbed a blueberry muffin, and we walked over to Grandpa's.

He lives about six blocks away from Dad in a little bungalow that he's tricked out with every possible kind of cabinet and storage closet, so many that I can't even imagine what he keeps in them all. Grandpa's a retired carpenter and cabinet-maker, specializing in fine wood built-ins for people with good taste and plenty of money. His own house is a symphony of magnificent woods, including some really nice pieces of furniture that he made himself. My favorite is his coffee table, inlaid with a pattern of mahogany, cherry, tulip, poplar, and black walnut.

But the house always seems sad to me since Grandma Madeline died. It feels so *empty*. I keep expecting her to pop around a corner and hold her arms out to give me a hug, to say, "My goodness, how you've grown!" It hurts like crazy to realize that I'll never hear her singing in the kitchen again, that her hugs are all gone. I never got nearly enough of them.

Grandpa seemed surprised to see us, and I realized that we'd never actually made a plan to meet him this morning.

"Gosh," he told us, looking a little concerned. "I just tried to call and tell you I couldn't help you with the treasure hunt today."

"How come?" Jason asked, sounding hurt.

"I talked to Carolyn a little while ago," he explained, "and she's agreed to take me on as an assistant till after the baby's born. I'm afraid she's working too hard. So I'm about to begin my on-the-job training." He pirouetted, and we all laughed. "Do I look okay?"

"Like a million bucks," Jason told him. Jason's become very money-conscious lately. Of course that's what Carolyn expects of him, but it also has my mom kind of worried. I heard her telling Nicholas not long ago that there are far too many ways a lazy kid who wants easy money can get in trouble.

"Tell you what," Grandpa went on. "It's a beautiful morning, and we could all use some exercise.

If you kids'll walk me over, we can plot strategy on the way."

This was not exactly how I'd envisioned the morning, and it was also turning into a lot more walking than I'd had in mind. It's a good mile from Grandpa's place to Carolyn's Gift Exchange. But I was hardly in a position to say no.

Grandpa set a lively pace, and Jason used his skateboard as a kind of scooter beside us. "So," Grandpa said as we passed a yard holding what looked like the world's largest Christmas tree, "we've got five clues left, right?"

"Four, really," I told him, "leaving out the one about the first name of the first female settler in Kontowoc County."

"What about the others?" Grandpa asked.

I looked down at the paper where I'd copied our remaining clues. "There's one about some woman who went west and had a song written about her."

Grandpa chuckled. "Music's not my strong suit. I couldn't carry a tune in an eighteen-wheeler. What else?"

"The one I spent so much time on yesterday," I told him, "about something changing colors. It's pink and changes to purple and then back to pink before it dies."

Jason made a big show of screeching to a stop. "I've got it!" he announced jubilantly.

"What?" Grandpa asked.

"It's Vangie's hair!"

Even I had to laugh at that one, and in fact the

streak today *was* violet. Actually, though I wasn't about to admit it right now, I was starting to get a little worried about the section of hair I kept spraying. It was kind of dingy when the colorings were washed away, and starting to get rather brittle.

Back to the subject at hand. "I thought about litmus paper," I told them, "but I don't know if they had litmus paper back then. You know any scientists, Grandpa?"

"Afraid not," he answered, shaking his head regretfully. "What else is there?"

"There's one about the Civil War and polecats," I answered.

He chuckled at that one. "Always did think the Confederates were a bunch of skunks. As it happens, I know just the person to ask about that. I'll call him tonight."

We turned a corner onto Central Avenue, where Carolyn's shop is located, about five blocks from the library. Grandpa suddenly seemed nervous, which struck me as odd. "All right, kids, we're almost there. What's the last one?"

I didn't even need to look at the list. "It's about food, or cooking. Something like that."

"Then you're in luck." He stopped and pointed across the street. "One of Carolyn's friends just opened her own restaurant."

Crêpes Suzette, it was called, a storefront with open shutters inside the front windows and an elegantly lettered sign hanging above the shutters. It was the most promising lead so far, I supposed, though we'd have to have Carolyn introduce us.

She was with a customer when we arrived. The customer looked around rather furtively at our entrance. "You're absolutely certain," she said softly to Carolyn, "that nobody will know who brought these things in here."

"We use numerical codes on the objects and *never* reveal the names of contributors," Carolyn assured her. She pointed to the Unique Nook in a back corner of the sales floor. Among other things, it featured a model of the U.S. Capitol with a barometer in the dome, a string of Christmas lights shaped like ears of corn, and a five-foot-tall Elvis floor lamp.

"Of course some items are one-of-a-kind," she went on. "But your daughter shouldn't worry about people recognizing their wedding gifts on our shelves. It just doesn't happen. Besides, you won't be bringing them in until after they've been displayed at the wedding."

The woman looked almost convinced, but she still averted her eyes from the three of us waiting in the store as she left.

Jason wandered into the Unique Nook and picked up a towel rack covered with seashells. It seemed an ignominious end for such beautiful ocean creatures.

Carolyn smiled at us all, looking a bit puzzled. "Goodness, an entire delegation! To what do I owe the pleasure?"

"They took pity on a nervous old man starting a new job," Grandpa said.

Carolyn laughed. "Well, make yourselves at home," she told us, "while I write up these things that just came in before that last customer." She looked at the pile: towels in assorted fluorescent colors, a Garfield clock radio, and four blenders. Then she smiled. "Actually, Ed, maybe we could wait a minute and I'll show you how that's done."

Jason and I kind of hung around while she gave Grandpa his orientation. I examined a teapot that was based on "The Old Woman Who Lived in a Shoe." It had little ceramic children hanging all over it, with the spout in the upturned toe. Way up on the lid, the old lady was giving one of the kids a spanking. I tried to imagine who would design such an object and who would buy it. Hopeless on both counts, though it was easy to understand how it had ended up here. Nobody in their right mind would ever want to *keep* it.

Finally there came a lull in Grandpa's on-the-job training course.

"Say, Carolyn," I began. She looked at me curiously. I don't initiate a lot of conversations with her, now that I think about it. "You remember that clue about food in the treasure hunt?"

She gave a little nod that suggested she didn't remember it at all. Well, she *had* been asleep when we finished last night.

"Well, Grandpa said that the restaurant across

the street belongs to a friend of yours, and we were wondering . . ."

She was nice enough to catch on immediately. "Why, that's a great idea! If anybody would know about food, it'd be Suzette." She looked at Grandpa. "If you wouldn't mind, Ed, I could take them over there now. Suzette will be getting ready for lunch, but maybe she'll have a spare minute. And it will be *much* harder for her to find time once the lunchtime customers start coming in."

Grandpa looked nervous. "Will you be gone long?"

"Only a few minutes," Carolyn promised. That didn't surprise me. I expected a fast drop-off and a speedy departure from her.

"Then go ahead," Grandpa said. "If I get in over my head, I'll open the front door and give my patented wolf howl."

The sign in the window at *Crêpes Suzette* said CLOSED, but Carolyn knocked sharply and after a moment a tiny woman came out of the back, frowning. She wore a tall white chef's hat and white apron over white pants and shirt. She broke into a smile when she saw Carolyn and hurried across the dining room.

"Why, hi!" she told us, unlocking the door and letting us in. Inside smelled *wonderful*. "C'mon in. You're a little early for lunch, but the soup's ready." Carolyn introduced Jason and me, and Suzette smiled. "I've heard *lots* about you," she told us.

I could just imagine.

Suzette turned to me. "*Great* hair, Vangie!" she said with what actually sounded like genuine enthusiasm. Finally, somebody appreciating individuality.

Carolyn, who these days never stayed on her feet a moment longer than necessary, pulled out a chair from one of the tables and sat down. Crisp white tablecloths covered all the tables, and little vases of real flowers sat in the middle of each one.

"The kids are involved in a kind of . . . well, I guess you could say it's like a scavenger hunt," Carolyn explained. "They need some information about food, and you know me. If you can't microwave it, I'm totally lost."

Suzette's brown eyes sparkled. There were wisps of curly brown hair escaping all around the bottom of her chef's hat. "Come on in the kitchen," she suggested. "I've got things on the stove I don't dare leave."

"I'd better get back," Carolyn told her, sidling toward the door. "My father-in-law's minding the shop, and it's his first day."

"Well, if the kids don't come right back," Suzette said, laughing, "it'll be because I've put them to work."

Suzette locked the door after Carolyn and led us to the back of the restaurant. The cooking aromas were even stronger here, and I felt suddenly ravenous. One blueberry muffin isn't really enough to fuel two brisk crosstown walks.

The kitchen was small, but it absolutely glittered. Everything was either pristine white or brightly polished metal. Some copper pans were hanging from the ceiling, and one whole wall was cookbooks.

Eureka! I thought. It's a great word, the state motto of California. It means "I have found it." I hoped we'd find it here.

Once in the kitchen, Suzette began doing about fourteen things all at once. She stirred several pots on the big stove, glanced at the clock, and started heating some olive oil in a frying pan the size of a small satellite dish. There were piles of chopped vegetables beside the stove: onions and eggplant and peppers and tomatoes. She dropped some garlic into the pan, and it began sizzling. I love the smell of cooking garlic.

"Okay," she said as she worked, "tell me what this riddle is that you need to solve."

I already had it out. "This is kind of goofy-sounding, but here goes:

> My properties make special food
> > From something which itself is good.
> A young one dies and that is how."

Suzette pushed the onions into the pan and stirred them with a big wooden spoon. "That's it?" she asked.

"That's it," I told her. I looked at Jason. He was hovering by the doorway and looked surprisingly uncomfortable. Or maybe just naked without his skateboard, which he'd left at Carolyn's shop.

Suzette added eggplant and peppers. "A young one dies," she said pensively. "Could it mean something like a suckling pig? Or veal?"

I thought with fleeting revulsion of the slaughter of calves for veal, one of the most hideous parts of the video that had turned me vegetarian.

But Suzette shook her head. "That doesn't make sense," she went on. "I don't think. There's all kinds of baby vegetables, of course. I suppose you could look through my cookbooks. . . ."

I caught Jason's eye as I turned to look at the formidable wall of cookbooks. It was daunting. If we had to read them all to find the clue, I could tell Jason was prepared to pack it in right now.

"But we don't know what we're looking for," Jason said.

"That would slow you down a bit, wouldn't it?" Suzanne agreed cheerfully. She was grating cheese now, stopping at intervals to stir the vegetables. If I didn't eat something soon, I might pass out. "How soon do you need to know this?"

Jason and I spoke in unison. "Tomorrow," I said. "Friday," he told her.

She gave a hearty laugh. "Just like my brother and me. Let's see now. It's something with *properties* which act on something else. Heat's a property that changes lots of things in cooking. So's micro-waving."

"I think we can rule out microwaving," I told her. "This clue was written before microwave ovens were invented. *Long* before."

"Then what else has properties that change food?" Suzette thought out loud. "Cold does. How about ice cream?"

I was horrified. "Does something *die* to make ice cream?" It was bad enough to give up cheese-burgers, but ice cream is one of my basic food groups.

"Only reducing plans," Suzette answered. "No, I guess that's not it. Now, emulsifiers change the properties of food. Egg yolks create an emulsion with oil to make mayonnaise, for instance. Mustard's another one, like in vinaigrette salad dressing. It keeps the oil and vinegar from separating. And of course there are scads of chemical emulsifiers, the ones with the long names you read in the fine print on convenience food packages."

"Definitely nothing involving convenience foods," I told her. Presumably home-canned okra didn't count.

"Or acidic foods," Suzette suggested. "Lemon juice curdles cream, for instance."

"I suppose that could be it," Jason said doubt-fully. About all he can manage to do in the kitchen is pour cereal or microwave hot dogs.

"Well, what about tools?" Suzette asked. "Like a food processor or a blender?"

"The riddle was written a hundred years ago," I told her. "I guess I should have made that clear."

Suzette shrugged. "Oh. Actually, that helps, narrows it down a bit. An eggbeater or a whisk? Mortar and pestle? How about a plain old knife? Its sharpness is a property, and that would fit with something young dying." She frowned. "This is really tough, you know? Maybe the angle to concentrate on is the something young that dies."

The back door opened, and a young woman in a waitress uniform came in. "Hi, Suzette," she said. "Menu ready for the blackboard?"

Suzette looked at her watch in horror. "Yikes! I'm way behind in everything. Listen, can I think about this for a day or two?"

"Sure," I told her, trying to hide my disappointment. And my hunger.

She smiled. "There's one thing you two could do for me," she said.

"What?" Jason asked suspiciously. I think he visualized himself up to his elbows in greasy dishwater.

"Try out this vegetable soup," Suzette told us with a grin. "If you happen to be hungry, that is."

"We happen to," I told her gratefully.

And the soup was delicious, served with some crusty, warm whole wheat rolls and the best salad I'd had since I left L.A. It contained several lettuces besides the usual Minnesota iceberg—Bibb, romaine, even a little bitter red radicchio.

Later on, I realized we were lucky to have stumbled on such a great meal.

Because the afternoon went straight downhill as soon as we got back to the library.

CHAPTER TEN

It wasn't until the next night that Grandpa was able to take us to see Colonel Hathaway, his friend who knew all about the Civil War. And the time we spent waiting was pretty depressing.

In a full afternoon's research at the library after lunch at *Crêpes Suzette*, Jason and I weren't able to solve any more clues. Oh, we did manage to check back on the moons of Jupiter, and sure enough, Dad was right. The last eight of them weren't discovered until after Langley Patterson put together his test. But even changing that TWELVE to FOUR didn't help us much. Now our letters were AIODWUMA. A real breakthrough.

Curiosity had gotten the better of me, however, and I checked out a copy of *Gone with the Wind* before we left. It was the longest book I'd ever considered reading, and I figured if I liked it, it should last through the rest of the summer. Which would take care of some of my what-to-do problems. Solving the treasure hunt wasn't likely to take up much more time, unless miracles started happening fast. And you can only work a bead loom for so long before it starts getting really tedious.

Colonel Hathaway's apartment building seemed an unlikely site for a miracle. It was an old red brick building in a Minneapolis neighborhood of similar apartments. He lived on the third floor, and there was no elevator. Not a good beginning.

The building had the strong, stale smell of old food, and the odors weren't nearly as inviting as the aromas in Suzette's restaurant.

"What *is* that smell?" Jason asked Grandpa as we trudged up the first flight of stairs.

He paused on the landing and gave an elaborate sniff. "One part last winter's cabbage, two parts last week's beets."

I recoiled, even though I do have a fondness for pickled beets. "Yuck!"

We climbed another flight, and Grandpa turned to us. "Now remember," he whispered, "best behavior. He can be a tad crotchety."

At Grandpa's first knock, the door swung all the way open. A tall man in khaki slacks and a crisply ironed shirt stared at us suspiciously. He was at least Grandpa's age, but he looked like those older guys you see running along the beach in little shorts. He probably spent three hours a day on the Life Cycle and would live to be a hundred.

"Good evening, Edwin," Colonel Hathaway said. His voice was brisk, no-nonsense. "Punctual as usual."

111

"You're looking well, Nathan," Grandpa answered formally. "These are my grandchildren, Jason and Vangie. They're visiting from California."

Colonel Hathaway looked at us as if we'd just crawled out from under a rock. He reserved a particular glare for the bright yellow streak in my hair. "Well, come in," he said, after a moment. "Edwin, you mentioned some kind of puzzle?"

"That I did," Grandpa told him, as Colonel Hathaway led us through a small, tidy living room into his office. It was a military history museum, every item in its precise place. Bookshelves were full of big fat history books, and Civil War pictures and maps covered the walls.

His desk sat in the absolute center of the room, a plain wooden one with two neat stacks of paper, one on either corner. Behind the desk stood a full-size American flag, and on the wall a framed official portrait of the president of the United States.

"You children studied the Civil War?" Colonel Hathaway asked as he took a seat behind his desk. He had three wooden chairs lined up facing the desk, and we sat in them.

I nodded, while Jason shook his head.

"When was Appomattox?" he barked at me.

I froze. I'm not much good at remembering dates under the best of circumstances, and as circumstances go, this was pretty far removed from best. "Uh . . ." I hesitated.

He looked at me with disgust. "April 9, 1865. That's what's wrong with today's schools. Everybody's shooting drugs when they ought to be drilling dates. Children used to learn every battle properly. Now it's just a disgrace."

I wanted to defend my school, which is actually quite good. And we'd studied the Civil War pretty thoroughly, too, just last year with Mr. Masterson, who's a really terrific teacher. But we spent more time concentrating on the issue of slavery than when each silly battle happened.

Grandpa intervened. "I'm not sure we can really hold Jason and Vangie personally responsible for the decline of American education, Nathan. If anything, they're innocent victims." He took out a card on which I'd written the Civil War clue and handed it to Colonel Hathaway. "Now, this is the puzzle question."

Colonel Hathaway frowned and read out loud:

"No polecat I, I tried to be
    An honor to Commander Lee
  Abroad returned from whence I came."

He furrowed his brow. "Not too many foreigners in the Confederate Army. Shouldn't be difficult to track down."

He reached into a bookcase, pulled down a large volume, and began examining it. Meanwhile, Jason stood up and crossed to an enormous Civil War map studded with pins and markers.

"This is a really neat map," Jason said politely. Colonel Hathaway looked up. "Oh yes, yes.

113

April of sixty-three right now. Change it every month." He returned his attention to the book, and a moment later found what he'd been looking for. He grunted in pleasure. "Umph. Here we go."

Jason scooted back to his chair and sat down, slouching. Grandpa gave him a look and he straightened up.

"Frenchman," Colonel Hathaway said. "Came to the Confederacy from the Crimean War. Fine record. Started as lieutenant colonel under Beauregard. Rose to general. Red River Campaign of sixty-four. Put in command of a brigade of Texans. Scruffy lot, didn't like him. Called him Polecat. Sounded kind of like his name."

I was mesmerized by this recitation. He was a fact machine, spitting out information. However, for all his fussing about educational standards, I didn't notice him using complete sentences to describe anything. Mrs. Hembree, my eighth-grade English teacher, marked off relentlessly for sentence fragments.

"Uh, what *was* his name, anyway?" Grandpa asked mildly.

Colonel Hathaway looked up with a glint in his eye. I don't know French, but it sounded to me like he was butchering the pronunciation. "Prince Camille Armand Jules Marie de Polignac."

"Wow!" said Jason involuntarily. "What a name!"

"French names all funny, seems to me," the Colonel answered. "Naming a boy Camille and Marie!

114

No wonder they're such sissified fighters. Want the rest?"

"Please," Grandpa said.

"Won the Texans over," Colonel Hathaway went on. "Must have been one heck of a CO. Moved up again. Went back to France in sixty-five trying to get money for the war effort. Not successful. Never came back. Only foreigner to gain high rank in the Confederacy."

"Could you write down his name for us?" I asked. Very politely.

"All of it?" Colonel Hathaway asked, taking a small pad of paper out of a drawer and beginning to write.

"Every last Camille and Marie," Grandpa assured him. "We really appreciate your help, Nathan."

Colonel Hathaway looked up and fixed a stony glance on Jason and me. We both hurried to add our thanks.

Mollified somewhat, Colonel Hathaway handed Grandpa the sheet of paper. "Anything else I can do for you?" he asked. "Just getting into a study of Vicksburg. Tremendous battle . . ."

Grandpa stood up and gave us the high sign to do likewise. With pleasure, I thought.

"I'm sure it's fascinating," Grandpa said mildly, "but I promised to get these kids back home at a respectable hour."

Colonel Hathaway rose, shook Grandpa's hand, and led us to the door. "Any time I can be of assistance," he offered, suddenly much friendlier. "School system needs all the supplementation it can get, that's what I always say."

Outside on the street, Jason began to laugh uncontrollably. In a moment, Grandpa and I joined in. We were practically rolling on the sidewalk.

"What does he *do* in there all day?" I wondered.

"I've often pondered on that question myself," Grandpa answered. "But let's not bite the hand that fed us. Or nibble on the brain that educated us. Most people's hobbies seem peculiar to somebody else. Skateboarding, for instance, strikes me as lunacy." He grinned as he got into the car. "The important part is, you kids got your answer, and there are only three clues left. What's on the agenda for tomorrow?"

"We still haven't heard back from Suzette," I told him. "So it's either the song or the changing colors."

"Hmmm," Grandpa said, as he pulled out into traffic. "I saw something in today's paper about a folk music festival this weekend. If you kids want, we could prowl around there a bit. And perhaps tomorrow we could go to the Science Museum."

Which we did. It was a fascinating place, with an Omnitheater that showed a feature which made me positively motion sick. But much as we enjoyed ourselves, we weren't any closer to figuring out Langley's color clue when we left.

"Maybe your dad will have an idea of somebody

who could help you kids," Grandpa suggested on the way home. "After all, there's plenty of folks at a hospital who know about science."

Like Larry Monroe. Dad took us with him to work the next morning and brought us down to Larry's office beside the main hospital laboratory. The lab was a busy place, full of technicians peering through microscopes and hurrying around with baskets of specimens. I didn't want to think too precisely about just what those specimens might be, or how they were collected.

Larry wore glasses, and his hair was combed over a bald spot that pretty much covered the whole top of his head. Still, he didn't seem particularly old, and he was very friendly.

"Your dad informs me that you're trying to solve a mystery about nineteenth-century science," he told us, making it sound like the most natural thing in the world.

"It was written in 1883," I told him. "Here's the clue."

He took it and read aloud:

> *"I start as pink, but change my hue*
> > *To purple as my life is through*
> *To pink once more, a final time.*

You know, this doesn't really sound much like chemistry. There are all sorts of compounds and reactions that change color, of course, but that reference to 'life' . . . I don't know. It sounds more like one of the biological sciences."

"Terrific," I muttered. Every time we managed to pry an informational door open, somebody slammed it in our faces.

"Don't look so glum," he told us. "My wife's a botanist at the conservatory. Maybe she can help."

Dad dropped us off after lunch at the conservatory where Barbara Monroe worked. It was a wonderful jungly place full of tropical and semitropical plants. A lot of them were things that grow outdoors in Southern California, sometimes wildly out of control. But here the climate is a lot more harsh. Indoors is the only place they can survive.

I liked Barbara right away, the same way I'd liked Suzette. She wore jeans and a planting apron and had a jillion freckles, which she didn't seem to mind at all. She wasn't wearing any makeup.

She led us along a stone path while we talked, picking off dead leaves and casually tending the plants as we went along.

"From pink to purple to pink in 1883?" she said, with a frown. "Do you have any idea what geographic area this might be?"

"Mississippi," Jason told her.

Her eyes widened. "Hmmm. That complicates matters considerably. So many things grow in the Deep South that we can only do up here in greenhouses."

"Couldn't it be some kind of flower?" I asked her.

"Sure. In fact, it probably *is* some kind of flower. Many flowers change hues as they go through their life cycles. And others change hues as they're exposed to direct sunlight."

"Then, isn't that it?" Jason wondered.

Barbara twisted a yellowed leaf off a shrub. I didn't know its name, but I recognized it as something that grows beside my friend Lauren's pool in L.A. "The problem is," she explained, "that there are thousands of species of flowers. For example, camellias are widespread in the South, and most of them are shades of pink. But there are *hundreds* of different camellias."

"Couldn't the answer just be 'camellia'?" I asked her.

"Certainly," Barbara answered. I brightened. But then she continued. "Of course, it could just as easily be azalea or wisteria or hemerocallis or rhododendron or clematis or hydrangea . . ." She shrugged her shoulders. "I'm not being much help, am I?"

"That's all right," I told her politely. "We never expected it to be easy."

But we hadn't expected it to be impossible, either.

CHAPTER
ELEVEN

Sunday afternoon we went to Callahan Park with Grandpa for the folk music festival. There were several small stages set up around the park, with simultaneous performances going on at each of them. The performers were casually dressed, most of them in jeans and T-shirts, accompanying themselves on acoustic guitars. A good-size crowd milled about, with people stopping here and there to sit on the grass in front of the different stages. I prefer rock and roll, myself, but some of this was kind of nice. Some of it was pretty raunchy, though, pure hillbilly sounds and people picking on banjos.

Grandpa led us over to an information booth. I'd put a glittering golden streak in my hair today, matching my gold spandex shorts and shoulder-length earrings, and it looked pretty terrific, I thought. I wasn't surprised that people stared—I'd gotten used to that, and actually kind of liked it— but it hurt my feelings when we passed a couple of teenage boys who pointed and laughed out loud. Obviously they were bumpkins.

A cheerful older woman with gray hair and glasses was at the information booth. Her name tag read MARTHA. "Can I help you?" she asked.

"I hope so," Grandpa told her. "We're looking for somebody familiar with the history of American folk music."

"Then you've come to the right place," Martha told him briskly.

"Does that mean you can help?" he asked.

"If it has to do with bluegrass or Appalachia, I'm your woman," she announced. With a start, I realized she was *flirting* with Grandpa. I looked at him with new eyes. If I were an old lady, would I find him appealing? The answer was a quick *yes*.

He smiled regretfully, and I realized that the flirting was going in two directions. Honestly!

"Unfortunately," he said, smiling broadly, "it doesn't. I need somebody who knows about music related to the westward expansion."

Martha thought for a minute, then beamed. "The best expert in that field's in Sweden right now, but Leon McAllister's here and he's a close second. He was over by that gazebo the last time I saw him." She pointed toward an open white building on the other side of the park. "Leon's a big fellow with a bushy beard. You can't miss him. He's pure country."

And indeed he was. He'd left the gazebo by the time we got there, but somebody pointed us in the right direction, and we caught up to him beside one of the small stages. Nobody was performing there at the moment.

Leon McAllister wore bib overalls and had a beard that sparrows could have nested in. Maybe even *were* nesting in. He looked like somebody you'd find holed up in a little log cabin that he'd built by hand on the side of a mountain. His accent was southern, but it was sharper than the Mississippi accents we'd heard in Prestonburg. He was, he told us, from the Ozarks, a hilly part of Arkansas and southern Missouri.

He sat on the edge of the stage and strummed his guitar thoughtfully. It had only taken one glance at the card for him to memorize what was on it. He probably knew a zillion song lyrics. " 'She headed west with lover bold,' " he said slowly, then strummed a mournful chord. " 'In search of California gold. Her journey's tale a song became.' " Another mournful chord. "A lot of songs came out of the west, a whole slew of 'em from the gold rush. 'Lulu,' for one."

He picked his guitar a moment, then sang:

> *"If you don't quit monkeying with my Lulu*
> *I'll tell you what I'll do*
> *I'll carve you up with my Bowie knife*
> *And shoot you with my pistol, too.*

Course, that don't really say much about the journey, or no lover, neither."

Jason caught my eye and rolled his eyes upward. I agreed that this guy was kind of peculiar, and his grammar was awful, but this was no time to be snobbish. I smiled sweetly at the man. He certainly seemed to know his stuff, and that was all we needed. Besides, Mom is forever reminding us that appearances don't count.

Leon McAllister thought some more, then started another song. "Frankie and Johnny were lovers . . ." He shook his head. "That wasn't California, though. Lovers, lovers . . . *her* lover . . . her lover, Ike? Of course!" He grinned and began to sing again:

"Oh, do you remember sweet Betsy from Pike
Who crossed the wide mountains with her lover Ike
With two yoke of cattle and one spotted hog
A tall Shanghai rooster and an old yellow dog.
Doodle da doodle da da da da doodle day."

"Betsy!" Jason and I shrieked in unison. "Betsy!"

Leon McAllister looked pleased. "That what you were looking for?"

"Oh yes, thank you!" I was so excited I almost hugged him. Then I realized that I didn't know him, and he was big and kind of weird, and we weren't in California, where everybody hugs everybody all the time automatically. I dropped my arms awkwardly to my sides.

"Yahoo!" Jason yelped, doing a fast spin down

the path on his skateboard. He nearly mowed down an elderly couple carrying banjos.

Grandpa looked chagrined. "How could I not remember 'Sweet Betsy from Pike'?"

And then things ground to a halt, for days. I spent quite a lot of time reading *Gone with the Wind*. The point of view was certainly different from the discussions we'd had in history class about the Civil War. I could almost understand the southerners' position, except, of course, for the part about owning slaves.

Owning slaves might be all right if you happened to be on the owning side, I supposed. But it seemed to me that your chances were just as good for *being* owned. And I had a very strong suspicion that even working for somebody as kind as Melanie Wilkes or Scarlett O'Hara's mother wouldn't make up for the fact that you couldn't just tell them to go take a flying leap and quit.

That you were stuck there, forever. *Forever.*

Still, I *did* like Scarlett. In her honor, I'd worn red streaks in my hair for several days now. She was just sixteen when the story started and I was about to turn fourteen, but she seemed *much* older, despite what everybody says about kids today growing up too fast.

I was also terrifically disturbed to discover that by Scarlett's standards, I was downright fat. I'm not overweight by any means, but my waist is a *lot* bigger than seventeen inches around. In fact, when

I put Carolyn's tape measure into a circle with a seventeen-inch circumference, it looked more like the waist of a newborn baby. The only parts of my body I could find that were seventeen inches around were my thighs.

I was filling in at Carolyn's Gift Exchange on Wednesday morning while Carolyn went to the obstetrician. Heaven knows, I didn't really want to be peddling excess food processors and serving trays covered with bunnies, but Carolyn was really wearing out easily these days, and I knew Dad was worried about her. Grandpa had thrown his back out the other afternoon, and Jason was over at his house, where they were going through Grandpa's fishing lures.

The store was pretty quiet. All I'd been doing for the past hour was reading *Gone with the Wind*, in fact. The battle of Gettysburg had just happened, and I felt really depressed. All those young men killed, and for what? Wars were so *stupid.*

The phone rang and a female voice asked for Carolyn.

"I'm sorry," I said, "she's not here right now. Could I help you with something?" Some king-sized bedsheets in puce, perhaps, or a can opener that plays "Yankee Doodle"?

"This is Suzette," the voice said. "Is that you, Vangie?"

I sat up straighter and looked out the front window. The CLOSED sign was still out on *Crêpes*

Suzette, but the lights were on. She must be in the back.

"It sure is," I told her. "Would you like me to have Carolyn call you?"

"Actually," Suzette said, "you're the one I'm looking for." I brightened. "I think I may have an answer to your riddle."

"You *do!*" I shrieked. "That's fantastic! What is it?"

"I'd rather tell you in person," she said. "There's something I need to show you to explain it. Is your grandfather there to watch the shop?"

"No," I told her, feeling like banging my fist on the counter. "He threw his back out. But I'll get Jason down here, and then as soon as Carolyn gets back from the doctor, we'll be right over." I hesitated. "I don't suppose you'd like to maybe give me just a teensy little hint?"

Suzette laughed. "I'll tell you everything when you get here. *Both* of you."

I hung up, called Jason, and told him to come on down, warp speed. And then I gave a scream of sheer delight.

Finally something was going our way!

Twenty minutes later, Carolyn had returned and Jason and I were in Suzette's kitchen. She was wearing her chef's whites again, standing beside a large colander filled with soft white cheese. The cheese was draining through cheesecloth into a bowl below.

"Twice a week," Suzette told us, "I make fresh cheese. I was watching the whey drain and suddenly it hit me. I realized the significance of what I was doing." She cocked her head. "Do you two know how cheese is made?"

We shook our heads.

"It's really very simple," she explained. "You mix milk with rennet, which solidifies the milk and separates it into curds and whey."

"Like Miss Muffet?" I asked.

"Exactly," she answered, with a little bob of her cap. "What I'm doing here is draining off the whey. But the important thing from your point of view is the rennet. Maybe you've even had rennet custard without realizing. Did you ever eat junket?"

Jason shook his head, but I remembered having it as a kid. "Yeah. It was like sweet solid milk."

"And very tasty, too," she said. "Rennet is what solidifies the milk. We buy rennet in tablets, made from rennin. And you know where rennin comes from?"

Again we shook our heads.

"Rennin," Suzanne announced triumphantly, "comes from the membrane that lines the fourth stomach of a calf!"

"Four stomachs?" Jason asked. He looked befuddled.

I felt suddenly ill. "The young one that dies," I said slowly.

"Exactly!" Suzette didn't seem to notice my dis-

127

tress. " 'My properties make special food'—that's cheese—'from something which itself is good'—milk. 'A young one dies and that is how'—the calf. Your answer's *got* to be rennet!"

It kept getting worse. "They kill calves to make cheese?" I asked slowly.

"She's a vegetarian," Jason explained, though I was certain I'd mentioned that to Suzette before, when we had lunch and I was checking that there was no beef in the soup. "Vangie the veggie."

Suzette patted my shoulder. "If it's any comfort, Vangie, a little rennet goes a long way. And there *are* synthetic versions of rennet, for vegetarian cheesemaking."

But it wasn't much comfort, not really. The next thing I knew, I'd be finding out that bing cherries were colored with pig's blood, or something equally disgusting.

Grandpa came over that night and we got out the Scrabble board. We took all the letters that we had found already and blanks for the two clues we were missing. Carolyn, on the couch, fell asleep almost instantly.

"But Dad," Jason argued, "we've solved all but two of them, and you said yourself we didn't have to find out that woman's name before we went back to Mississippi."

"There's still that other one you haven't solved," Dad pointed out. He was using his let's-all-be-reasonable-about-this tone. I hate that tone.

"Not 'cause we haven't tried," I argued. "And tried hard. I've spent days in the library and I can still smell that disgusting lab at the hospital."

Dad shook his head. "You're really putting me on the spot, kids. I never . . ." he hesitated.

"You never thought we could do it," Jason said angrily.

Dad looked embarrassed enough to make it clear that Jason was right. "Of course I thought you could," he maintained heartily.

Yeah, right. "And you promised that you'd take us back to Mississippi if we did. We might *never* be able to solve the last clue, Dad. Even a career botanist thought it was hopeless."

"Vangie," Dad said slowly, "there's no guarantee that we'd ever find anything if we went back down there. Clues or no clues."

I looked him right in the eye. "You always said there was nothing wrong with failing as long as you really, really tried."

He flinched and I knew I'd gotten to him. Cornered, he looked around for help. Carolyn was softly snoring, and Grandpa gave a big old grin.

"Don't look to me for help, son." Grandpa leaned back in his chair, still grinning. His back was much better, thank goodness. "I'm on their side. In fact, I'm half tempted to offer to lead the delegation."

Dad frowned. "But you haven't found anything on the Mississippi map that corresponds to the letters you have." He waved a hand at the Scrabble letters on the coffee table.

"It's not a very detailed map, Ron," Grandpa told him. "And maybe it's not old enough, either. Things change over the course of a century."

This time it was Dad who grinned. "Obviously your memory of Prestonburg is hazy, Dad. I don't think anything ever changes there." He looked around at all of us. "But all right. I can tell when I'm licked."

And that was that.

Except for later that night, after we'd all gone to bed. Dad and Carolyn were in their room, arguing. I couldn't make out words, but the tone was definitely angry. All of a sudden, Carolyn seemed to be wide-awake. I had a feeling that the argument was about the trip to Mississippi, and I opened my door just a fraction of an inch. Across the hall, their door was open several inches, and I could hear them quite clearly now. I sat on the floor just inside my room and eavesdropped shamelessly.

"Just because they're accustomed to having that psychiatrist stepfather indulge their every whim doesn't mean we have to try to compete financially," Carolyn said furiously.

"Oh, c'mon." Dad was trying to placate her, using the let's-be-reasonable tone. "The bed-and-breakfast place is cheap, and Dad will pay his own way. Besides, if you and I don't go, it'll cost even less."

Let's-be-reasonable didn't seem to work any better on Carolyn than it did on us. I found that vaguely cheering.

"I can *guarantee* I'm not going," Carolyn told him. "And you've already used up all your vacation time."

"So we stay home. Alone. Is that so terrible? I'd think you'd be jumping at the chance to get Vangie out of your hair for a few days."

How *dare* he? I was furious to think he wanted us gone. After all the reassurances that he loved having us visit. Four-bedroom house, *ha!* But mad as I was, I also felt vindicated. I knew now that she *did* complain about me behind my back. Probably nonstop.

"Please don't mention hair," Carolyn answered wearily. "I keep telling myself that puberty doesn't last forever. But that's not really even the point. It's such a wild goose chase."

"We don't know that." Dad surprised me, taking our side in the argument when he'd been arguing just the opposite earlier. "Langley *did* go west for ten years. He could easily have made some kind of fortune. There were gold mines, silver mines, copper mines . . ."

"Swell," Carolyn said disgustedly. "A big pile of pennies."

"But that's not really the point, hon. The kids have really tried. They've put a remarkable amount of time and energy into this, and it wouldn't be fair to stop them so close to the finish." The fact that he was defending us now helped, but I wasn't ready to forgive him yet, not by a long shot.

"Even if it turns out to be nothing?"

Dad's voice got very pious. "There's nothing wrong with failing," he began, but then he was cut off suddenly.

The next thing I knew, I could hear both of them laughing. I closed my door silently and went back to bed, feeling exhilarated and wide awake.

We just might do it after all.

As outrageous as this whole thing was, we might be within spitting distance of finding a genuine buried treasure. I wanted to squeal with glee, but I settled for a couple more chapters of *Gone with the Wind*.

CHAPTER TWELVE

We never did manage to solve the clue about the changing colors. Which meant we hadn't technically met the terms of our agreement with Dad, that he'd send us back if we solved all but the one last clue.

But finally, I think, we just wore him down. We had, after all, done everything that any of us could think of to find the answer. And so, after endless discussions, he agreed that we could go back to Mississippi.

I didn't think that August could be any hotter or stickier than June in Prestonburg, but I was wrong. The whole town was like a steam bath when Grandpa and Jason and I arrived a week later.

We were intending to maintain a low profile while we did our final research and sought out the treasure, but there were some big problems with that plan. First, anything that a member of the Bradley family did in Prestonburg was *major* news. They'd run a picture of our whole family on page one of the local newspaper after our last visit.

And second, Grandpa turned out to be the World's Most Eligible Bachelor.

This notion of Grandpa as ladies' man really floored me. I mean, it had been a couple of years since Grandma died, and I knew he missed her a lot. And Dad and Carolyn had alluded to the fact that he was quite popular at church socials and other functions in Marshfield.

But *still!* It was as if we'd arrived with Rhett Butler himself.

Certainly we'd noticed that there seemed to be an exceptionally large number of widows and elderly spinsters in Prestonburg on our earlier trip. But it never occurred to me that a good-looking and available older man would practically have to beat off eager women with a broom.

Under other circumstances, it would have just been quite silly, I suppose, and maybe even rather charming. But it interfered seriously with our freedom to move around on the sly. A comparable situation might have been my showing up for the first day of high school with Larry Turner and his Samoyeds, fresh from the set of "Wellington's World."

It started before we even got out of our rental car—an unobtrusive Ford sedan this time—at Miss Farnsworth's Bed-and-Breakfast. "Now remember," Grandpa was saying, "we don't want anyone to get suspicious. In a town like this, somebody on the north side gets an itch, a south-sider's right there to scratch it."

But he hadn't even finished speaking when Miss

Farnsworth came bouncing down the front steps like an NBA basketball player. "Why, your plane must've gotten in early," she burbled. "Hello, Vangie, Jason. And you must be Mr. Bradley's father . . ."

Grandpa extended a cordial hand. "Edwin Bradley." He glanced at the sign hanging on her porch. "Miss Farnsworth, I presume?"

Miss Farnsworth fluttered her lashes, and Jason rolled his eyes skyward.

"I can't begin to tell you how pleased we all are to be able to show you the restoration on Miss Griselda's house," she simpered. "I understand your late wife was her niece."

"That's right," Grandpa answered. "But I'm sorry to say that when Madeline and I came to Prestonburg, Miss Patterson refused to see us."

Jason had the bags out of the trunk by now, and he and Grandpa each carried one up the steps.

"I think I can safely guarantee you'll find the town more hospitable this time around," Miss Farnsworth assured him, holding the door open. *Very* hospitably.

And she was certainly right. When we got to Miss Griselda's house half an hour later, there was a waiting delegation of Historical Society ladies. The place itself had been really spiffed-up, with a fresh coat of paint outside and some marigolds blooming along the front walk. It also sported a new sign on its lawn, reading KONTOWOC COUNTY HISTORICAL SOCIETY.

Jason split pretty quickly, off to join the kids who were waiting expectantly for him and his skateboard outside Miss Griselda's house when we arrived. I stayed with Grandpa in the parlor, which had been scrubbed and freshened and polished. A window air conditioner was a welcome addition, and there were vases of flowers all over the place. A quick tour after we arrived showed that everything had been thoroughly cleaned, though they'd left Philip Patterson's pj's lying on the bed in his bedroom. Creepy.

We all sat around drinking lemonade and eating cookies: Grandpa, Miss Farnsworth (who had attached herself to Grandpa like a fluffy white-haired barnacle), Miss Lavinia and Miss Estelle Tuthill, and Clara Clifton, Mr. Winthrop the Elder's sister.

Grandpa seemed to be thoroughly enjoying himself. "That many people take your azalea festival tours?" he asked in wonder.

"Some years we have to close off reservations a month before the festival even begins," Mrs. Clifton told him proudly.

"It should be easier to manage," Miss Lavinia noted, "now that we have this wonderful facility in town."

"Will this house be part of the tour now?" Grandpa asked.

The women murmured among themselves a moment. Apparently this was a touchy subject.

Finally Miss Farnsworth spoke. "We haven't decided just how to handle that yet. We've shown the place to interested townspeople, of course, but we weren't sure how your son would feel . . ."

"I'm sure Ron will be honored to share his heritage," Grandpa assured her. I wanted to barf.

We ate an early dinner at Miss Farnsworth's that night: fried chicken, hush puppies, okra, and iced tea. It wasn't exactly an easy meal for a vegetarian, since the only salad was an orange Jell-O mold with coconut and mandarin oranges in it. The okra was fried and not quite so slimy, but I could still barely choke it down. I stayed polite, however.

Miss Farnsworth was all atwitter. "I can't get over how many of my own rules I've broken today," she confided. "Serving an evening meal to guests, sitting down at table with them . . ."

Grandpa Gallant jumped right in. "We couldn't very well let you fix such a fine meal and not share it."

Jason smothered a gagging noise and held up a hush puppy on his fork. "Why are these things named after shoes?" he asked.

Miss Farnsworth laughed merrily. "These hush puppies came long before the kind you wear, Jason. They used to toss them to the dogs when they were barking, to get them to quiet down."

"Seems like a waste of fine food," Grandpa told her.

And so it went, clear through dessert, which turned out to be a choice of blueberry cobbler or cherry pie. Democratically, I took both.

And when Grandpa went out on the porch for

coffee with Miss Farnsworth after dinner, Jason and I retreated to our bedrooms upstairs. Enough was enough.

The next morning we began our research in earnest. We strolled on down to Miss Griselda's house, where Jason once again hit the street with his skateboard for his collection of young fans.

Grandpa had, the day before, professed a fascination with the early history of Kontowoc County, making up some kind of nonsense about comparing it to the settlement of Minnesota. Not that an excuse was really necessary. He could have told the Historical Society ladies he wanted to compare local history to weather patterns in the Sahara or pygmy migrations in the rain forest, and they'd have cheerfully offered to help.

Miss Lavinia Tuthill, it developed, was the most dedicated historian, a former high school social studies teacher. She volunteered to assist. I sat in the corner of Philip Patterson's former office with *Gone with the Wind*, a reading choice that had not gone unremarked by the ladies. Scarlett had just married Frank Kennedy, which I considered a major blunder.

"This is the oldest map I can put my hands on," Miss Lavinia told him, "from 1897." Grandpa sat at a small table which had been brought in to replace the huge rolltop desk now sitting in Dad and Carolyn's living room in Minnesota. "We lost a lot of our older materials in the flood of fifty-eight."

Grandpa smiled encouragingly at her. The fool! She'd never leave at this rate. "Should be more than adequate for my simple curiosity, Miss Lavinia. And these are the local history books?" He indicated a section of the room's shelving where the rocks had been replaced by a collection of elderly-looking volumes. The rocks that remained had been consolidated somewhat, and dusted thoroughly.

"That whole second shelf," she told him. "Could I help you find something?"

"Not really," he answered. "Like I told you, I'd just like to get a little sense of where we are. My Madeline was always interested . . ."

"I'm so *sorry* your late wife never got to see this lovely home," Miss Lavinia told him. "Now don't get so caught up in your studies that you forget lunch with Estelle and myself!"

Finally, after a lot more fussing around, she left us alone. Grandpa pulled down a volume and examined it.

"*Our Gallant Forebears* by Langley Patterson. Handwritten, I'm afraid." He looked at me and winked. "But at least it's not in verse!"

An hour and a half later, Grandpa looked up at me and grinned. "Hope," he said.

"I *am* hoping," I shot back, "and I have been for weeks."

He laughed. "That wasn't an instruction, Vangie.

It was your answer. The wife of the first white settler in Kontowoc County was named Hope LeFarge."

I looked around quickly to be sure no Historical Society ladies were lurking nearby, then looked at him in amazement. "Hope," I said slowly. "Hope. You know, Grandpa, that's almost like a sign we're going to succeed."

"Well," he said slowly, "we can *Hope* so."

That afternoon we huddled in my bedroom at Miss Farnsworth's Bed-and-Breakfast, with the door closed and the air conditioner set to HIGH. I got out the Scrabble letters.

Lunch had been another massive meal. Grandpa burped contentedly. "I guess they haven't heard of cholesterol yet in these parts."

"You're gonna *really* look like Santa Claus by the time we go home," Jason chided him. "I can't believe the way those ladies keep feeding you!" He took a brownie from a plate that had appeared miraculously in my room while we were gone.

"Men don't get doted on nearly enough these days, Jason," Grandpa told him with a grin. "Now here's Langley's instruction:

> *Now take these letters you have found*
> *And move them carefully around.*
> *A name they'll make in proper order*
> *A site within the County border."*

"It's a big county," Jason noted glumly. "And what if the place is a parking lot now or something?"

"Langley Patterson didn't know when his letter would be found," Grandpa reminded him. "He probably picked a place that he expected to stay the same for a while."

"That he *hoped* would," Jason answered with a giggle. By now we'd made every bad joke imaginable that you could base on the word *hope*.

I separated out the letters that we needed: *H, C, O, W, U, M, N, D, T, I*, two *A*s and a blank.

"Finding Hope gave us *H*," I said. "Tell me some place on the map and I'll see if the letters fit."

Grandpa carefully opened the Kontowoc County map he had borrowed from Miss Griselda's house. "Let's try geographic landmarks," he suggested. "They don't change over time. There's the Kontowoc River . . ."

"Wrong letters," I told him.

"Natchez Trace?"

"Nope."

"Caltamount Ridge?"

"No."

He started reading faster now, not waiting for my response. "Prestonburg Creek? Wentworth Plantation? Chinataw Mound? Carter Hall?"

"Wait a minute!" I held up a hand to stop him. "Go back! What was that last one?"

"Carter Hall?"

"No, before that."

"Chinataw Mound."

"Spell it!" I ordered.

"C-H-I-N-A-T-A-W-M-O-U-N-D."

As Grandpa read the letters, Jason and I picked them up and placed them in order on the bed.

"That's it!" Jason squealed, his voice betraying him again.

"What is it?" I vaguely remembered seeing the sign on the outskirts of town when we'd driven in.

"It's an Indian mound, I believe," Grandpa answered.

"What's an Indian mound?" Jason asked.

"Indian mounds are found all over the country," Grandpa said. "They were the sites of various rituals, centuries ago. There's a park in Minneapolis with mounds that were probably built as burial sites for Sioux chieftains. It overlooks the Mississippi River, by the state fish hatchery."

Jason could barely contain himself. "So let's go!" he urged, jumping up.

Grandpa held up a warning hand. "Hold your horses, son! We're a little too conspicuous around here to just shoot out of town like that. We'd be leading a parade."

"But we've gotta go there!" Jason was bouncing around now, so excited he couldn't even stand still. "I can't wait."

"You're going to have to," Grandpa told him. "Our best bet is early morning, when nobody will be around."

I had an awful feeling about what this meant. "You mean like eight?" I asked.

"I mean like four-thirty," Grandpa told me.

CHAPTER
THIRTEEN

It was still dark when the three of us sneaked down the stairs and out to the rental car in the morning. I couldn't figure out how Jason and Grandpa managed to be so perky. I could barely move, and I wished I had toothpicks to prop my eyes open.

Nobody was out anywhere. It was the first time I'd seen the streets of Prestonburg empty. The car engine positively roared when Grandpa started it, and I was sure that windows would go flying up all around us. But nobody seemed to hear, and we quickly drove off.

Grandpa was oddly chatty. "You know, kids," he told us as we headed down the quiet street, "this has been a lot of fun, solving all the clues and coming down here and all. I'm really proud of both of you, working so well together. But I don't want you to be too terribly disappointed if we don't find anything."

"Oh, we won't be," Jason assured him, with false bravado.

But I knew Jason had his heart set on finding a treasure, and for that matter, so did I. It would be hideously disappointing if all this had been for nothing. The night before, as I tried to get to sleep early in anticipation of our predawn departure, I'd been fearful that the whole thing was madness. Even though it would make a great story to tell my friends back home. Not to mention any teachers who might want an essay on "How I Spent My Summer Vacation."

"In any case, it should be interesting," Grandpa went on cheerfully. "According to the Historical Society records I checked yesterday afternoon, this Indian mound was begun sometime between the years 1300 and 1600. The Indians who lived there were part of the Natchez, Creek, or Choctaw tribes, though nobody's really sure."

"What happened to them?" Jason asked.

"They died or left not long after Europeans began passing through this area," Grandpa answered. "De Soto found lots of natives in the 1540s, but by the time the French came in 1700 or so, most of them were gone."

"Shades of the Carolina parrot," I said darkly. "They probably died of measles or some other disease they got from de Soto." Jason looked puzzled. "That's what happened to most of the North American Indians," I told him. It was one of the more depressing details of American history class. "The Europeans didn't *have* to shoot them. We just gave them stuff like chicken pox and mumps. And wiped out whole tribes."

We drove along in silence, then, till we reached the turnoff to Chinataw Mound, where the road became narrow and winding. It led, after what felt like a million miles, to a clearing with a small parking lot.

Ahead sat the mound, just visible in the lightening sky, and it was curiously disappointing, just a neatly shaped grass-covered hill, somewhat flattened on the top. It was probably about forty feet in diameter.

"This is it?" Jason asked, with obvious surprise.

"Did you expect a neon sign saying TREASURE HERE?" I asked him irritably.

"Easy does it," Grandpa told me mildly. "We've gotten along so far. Let's not get cranky now. Vangie, you bring the instructions, and let's go. Are we supposed to start on top of the mound?"

"It doesn't say," I told him. I didn't need to look at the instruction sheet. I'd long since committed the rest of it to memory. Not that there was that much left.

"Then let's assume we should," he decided.

The mound was taller and rose at a much sharper angle than it had appeared from the car. The three of us stumbled awkwardly up its steep sides, scrabbling not to slide right back down again. Once Grandpa lost his balance, and Jason had to grab his arm to keep him from falling backwards.

"Not as limber as I once was," Grandpa muttered, mostly to himself.

Now we were on top of the mound. I looked around slowly, scanning the horizon for a full 360 degrees, then began to recite the instructions:

"There stand and look round thoroughly
And find two giant live oak trees.
Walk 'tween them then, your paces measure.
At 118 there lies the treasure."

I looked around again. Live oaks are enormous trees, and many of those in town were festooned with Spanish moss. At one point in the slow circle I made, I saw a single live oak. A single huge tree, at any rate.

Nowhere, however, were there two.

"Where *are* they?" Jason asked, an air of desperation in his voice.

Grandpa squinted, then pointed to a small, vine-covered mound about twenty feet away from the single big tree. "What about that? Could it be a stump?"

Jason immediately began to scramble down the side of the mound. "C'mon!" he urged.

"You kids go," Grandpa suggested. He was still a little winded from climbing up the side of the mound. "If that's it, don't forget that we have to pace it off from up here."

Jason got to the bottom of the mound seconds before I did, and the two of us raced in a dead heat across the grass. We reached the small clump of vines at the same time, and Jason began frantically pulling some of them away.

I hesitated. There seemed an excellent chance that little creatures might be living in there, and it was so early in the morning that they'd probably all be home.

By the time I made my first tentative swipe at the vines, Jason had already uncovered evidence of a stump. A very large stump.

"We found it!" Jason shouted back to Grandpa.

"Eureka!" I added.

Up on top of the mound, Grandpa beamed and raised both hands over his head, fists clenched. Slowly he began pacing and counting as he backed down the steep side of the sloping mound. When he reached the bottom he turned and began walking *ever* so slowly toward us.

"A-nine and a-ten and an-eleven and a-twelve," he announced as he made his leisurely way across the grassy field that separated us.

"Come *on!*" Jason yelled.

But I was suddenly nervous. And I realized that Grandpa wasn't going slowly just to torture us—though certainly that was part of it, probably a big part—but also because he was afraid there'd be nothing at the rainbow's end.

Grandpa smiled and began goose-stepping briskly, like a Nazi soldier in a World War II documentary. "Thirteen, fourteen, fifteen, sixteen . . ."

He stopped abruptly and put a hand tentatively behind him, feeling his lower back.

Oh, no!

If he'd thrown his back out horsing around, we were doomed. We'd have to give up on the treasure hunt, at least for now, while we tried to get him back to the car. Then we'd have to try to drive back to town, even though neither Jason nor I know anything about driving. Or we could wait till somebody else showed up, some passing tourist interested in Indian mounds. Or one of us could hike back to town and get help.

All three were extremely unappealing prospects.

Then Grandpa started forward again. No more fooling around, but he was walking steadily, and it didn't look like it particularly hurt him. Now he counted in a normal voice, however, and just walked.

And walked. And walked. And walked.

You would not *believe* how long 118 paces can take to walk. Or to watch someone walk.

By the time he got within a few yards of the tree and the stump, he was at one-twelve. Jason and I stationed ourselves midway between the tree and stump, urging him on.

"One-fourteen, one-fifteen, one-sixteen, one-seventeen, one-eighteen." Grandpa stopped and looked at his feet. "This is it! 'At one-eighteen there lies the treasure.' "

I recited the next part from memory:

"There find a small and hidden hole
    When you away a large stone roll."

We all looked around the ground expectantly.

No large stone. No medium stone. Not even a pebble.

The grass was pretty thick and about eight inches tall. Jason dropped to his hands and knees and began patting the earth, feeling around, going back toward the mound. He moved frantically, and I hoped he wouldn't have any unpleasant surprises, like meeting a snake family or sticking his hand into an anthill.

"Maybe my pace was shorter than his," Grandpa said, frowning. "Or longer. Folks are taller these days." He walked slowly forward, feeling the earth with his toe.

Then Jason gave a yell. "Here! Here's a rock!"

I ran over. Grandpa moved pretty quickly, too.

Jason was ripping heavy grass away from a flat stone about fifteen inches in diameter.

Grandpa pulled a pink-handled garden trowel out of one of his jacket pockets. "Not really the most appropriate tool, but it was all I could find in Mildred's potting shed."

Mildred? Since when was he calling Miss Farnsworth Mildred?

Grandpa used the trowel to loosen the dirt around the edges of the stone. It didn't look like it had been disturbed for a long, long time. Maybe even a hundred years.

Finally he had the stone loosened. "See if you two can pull it out," Grandpa suggested, "and spare my poor back."

Jason took one side of the stone, and I wedged my fingers under the other. We twisted it from side to side to help loosen it some more, then with a mighty effort heaved it upward and off the ground.

There was nothing underneath it.

Just dirt, plain old dirt. And it, too, looked like it hadn't been disturbed in a very long time.

"There's nothing here." Disappointment echoed in Jason's voice.

Grandpa handed me the trowel with a flourish. "Only one way to be sure of that. Go for it, Vange."

I dropped to my knees, grateful to be wearing jeans, and began digging. Miss Farnsworth's pink garden trowel was not a particularly effective tool. In fact, it was a perfectly ridiculous tool.

Jason knelt beside me and began scrabbling in the ground, digging out dirt with his bare hands, like a dog burying a bone. We quickly hit on a system: I'd plunge the trowel in fairly deeply and loosen the soil, and he'd help scoop it with his hands. Too bad Mildred Farnsworth didn't have *two* pink trowels.

We'd removed about a foot and a half of soil, and I was about ready to give up. Then I stuck the trowel its full depth into the ground to begin on another layer.

And hit something!

"Hey!" I hollered, frantically wiggling the trowel over the spot where it had struck. Jason began moving in triple time, and a few moments later we'd removed enough dirt to see that there was some kind of metal box in the hole.

We couldn't tell how big it was, so we started digging out toward the sides. Before long, we knew it was a foot square.

Then we started down the sides, digging out dirt alongside the box. I sure hoped it wasn't buried pointing down, whatever it was.

But it was only about nine inches deep. Time seemed to be standing still as we dug and scooped, but it probably only took a few minutes to clear enough dirt from the sides to be able to wiggle the box.

To wiggle . . . and then dislodge it.

It felt surprisingly light, and moved remarkably easily. Which meant, I realized quickly, that we hadn't unearthed any Confederate gold. Surely he wouldn't have buried Confederate *currency*, would he? That had been worthless for years by the time Langley Patterson made up his treasure hunt.

When it was clear that the box was loose and that it wasn't horrendously heavy, I let Jason finish. It took him very little effort to pull it the rest of the way out. He set it on the ground and we all stared at it for a moment, speechless.

It had once been painted a shiny black. Now the paint was missing in patches, and where the paint was gone, moisture had rusted its surface. On one side of the box was a metal clasp. Closed tightly by a padlock.

Grandpa scratched his head. "I'll be doggoned," he said in a tone of frank amazement. "I don't think I ever really believed there'd actually be anything here." He looked from me to Jason. "Who's got the key?"

Jason pulled the key that had been in the envelope out of his pocket with a triumphant wave. He knelt in front of the box and put the key into the lock. He simulated a drum roll: "Dum da da da dum . . ."

The key fit, but it wouldn't turn.

"I'm afraid it'll break if I try too hard," Jason said after a moment, looking to Grandpa for guidance.

Grandpa pulled a can of WD-40 out of another pocket and sprayed the lock. "We need to wait a moment or two to loosen this up," he apologized. "Anybody heard any good jokes lately?"

"Well, there's the one about the family who went to Mississippi looking for buried treasure," I told him. "But I don't know the punch line."

He gave a politely appreciative laugh, but after that nobody seemed to want to talk.

I sat down on the rock we'd moved and stared at the little metal box. What was inside it might change our lives.

After what seemed like an eternity later, Grandpa spoke up. "Let's give it another try, Jason. And really go for it this time. If we break the key, we'll buy a crowbar. That whole lock setup doesn't look like it was really meant to keep anybody out. It looks pretty symbolic to me."

Jason obediently twisted hard. I thought I saw the key bending, but then suddenly the lock popped open.

This time, Jason finished the verbal drum roll: "Dum da da da dum dum DUM!" Then he waved a gracious hand at me, a signal that I could open the box.

Slowly I lifted the lid.

CHAPTER
FOURTEEN

I blinked as I looked into the box, trying to figure out what it was.

Then I blinked again.

Shoes.

Disgusting shoes.

They were covered with grayish white mildew and patches of awful green mold. The same moisture that had rusted the sides of the box had seeped inside and grown hideous organisms all over the shoes.

I automatically recoiled. Jason, who usually makes a point of liking yucky nature-type things that bother me, didn't seem too keen on picking them up either. He looked around, found a stick, and used it to push them carefully aside in the box.

"Anything else in there?" Grandpa asked.

While Jason poked around, I took a closer look at the shoes. Not *too* close, mind you, but close enough to identify them as old-fashioned, high-topped shoes that had probably started out black. They buttoned up the sides and had extremely pointy toes and funny little hourglass-shaped high heels.

It was hard to contain my disappointment. Was *this* what we'd come so far to find? What we'd spent those long hours researching and trying to solve esoteric nineteenth-century puzzles for? It hardly seemed fair.

Jason gave a little yelp and came up with something on the end of his stick.

Bracelets! Two of them.

They were a pair. Jason held the stick out to me, and I tentatively removed one. It was gold, inlaid with onyx. As I turned it over, I caught sight of faint engraving inside.

I peered more closely at the engraving. " 'To Anna from Langley with love.' " I frowned. "Who was Anna?"

Grandpa chuckled. "Not his wife. Very interesting . . ."

Jason kicked the flat stone we'd removed to get at the box. "This isn't a treasure!"

"The bracelets might be valuable," Grandpa observed.

"But not worth *that* much," I told him. If they were solid gold, of course, they'd be worth a fair amount on sheer weight alone. And they presented a mystery of their own, about Anna's identity. But *still*. "I guess," I said slowly, "that when we actually found a box here, I was expecting more."

"Maybe there's something in the shoes," Grandpa suggested.

"Spiders, probably," I told him.

But Jason's curiosity was piqued. He looked at the shoes, started to touch them, then had an apparent brain wave. He hurriedly removed one of his shoes and took off his sock, putting his hand inside it. Then he cautiously inserted his hand into first one shoe and then the other.

His face showed clearly that they were empty.

"Do the heels come off?" Grandpa wondered.

Jason wiggled the heels and nothing happened. Then he tossed the shoes back in the box and peeled the sock off his hand. He started to put it back on, looked at it a moment, then threw it into the hole. He stuck his shoe on over his bare foot and started angrily kicking dirt back into the hole.

"Disappointing though this may be," Grandpa said, "I assume we're going to take everything back with us."

"Sure," I told him, closing the box. But I let Jason carry it.

We drove back into town in dispirited silence. Prestonburg was starting to wake up. There was a young woman out jogging, pushing one of those three-wheeled baby strollers, just like the young moms do back in L.A. It seemed a strange link to home.

We got to Miss Farnsworth's and found her waiting anxiously on the porch.

"Why, there you all are!" she said, looking upset. "I was about to call the sheriff on you. I thought you'd been kidnapped or something."

"Just out for an early morning drive," Grandpa told her cheerfully. "Working up an appetite for breakfast." He had wrapped his jacket around the box and carried it nonchalantly right past her, up the stairs, and into the room he and Jason were sharing.

"Breakfast in ten minutes!" Miss Farnsworth called after us.

Grandpa carefully closed the room door behind us and put the little hook into the eye to lock it. Some security system. Then he carried the box into the bathroom and set it in the tub.

"We can't very well take these home in this condition," he said. "Might as well take a stab at cleaning everything up a bit." He set the shoes under the tap in the bathtub and turned on the water gently.

"You think Dad's gonna be mad that we went to all this trouble for nothing?" Jason asked from the doorway.

I thought about it a minute. "Nah. But I bet Carolyn'll know to the penny how much we wasted coming down here." I shrugged. "So she'll have to sell some more Egyptian-style dental floss dispensers." I wasn't feeling very charitable toward anybody right now.

I sat on the edge of the tub and looked down at the shoes. Where the stream of water was hitting them, the gook was washing off and showing black leather.

But something else was happening. I leaned closer.

The water was splashing directly on the buttons on one side of the right shoe. Little bits of paint were flaking off them.

For the first time, I noticed that the buttons didn't precisely match each other. Some were round, others were square, and the one under the water was oval.

An oval that was now glittering as the water cascaded off it.

Glittering!

"Hey!" I yelled. "Look at this!"

I picked up the shoe, not even thinking about the mold of the ages or anything but that strange glittering oval. I rubbed the last flecks of paint off it. It looked like . . . a diamond.

A diamond?

I stuck the shoe back under the water, leaned forward and rubbed at the other buttons. The paint came easily off them, too. Some were green, others were red, and several more were clear.

Emeralds.

Rubies.

Diamonds.

We actually *had* found a treasure!

Jason and I let out huge screams at the same time.

"I'll be darned," Grandpa said, taking the shoe out of my shaking hand.

Without even thinking about it, I got up and gave Jason a mighty hug. We shrieked again.

Moments later, while we were still hollering and carrying on, a loud knock came at the door.

"Is everything all right in there?" Miss Farnsworth's voice came clearly across the room. Thank heavens we'd put on the lock.

We all looked at each other and began laughing uproariously. Yes indeed, I'd say everything was all right.

"What's going *on?*" Miss Farnsworth called.

"Oh, we're just washing up," Grandpa called back. "Just washing up!"

And we rolled on the floor, convulsed in laughter.

Well, you can just imagine how difficult it was to act like nothing had happened for the rest of our time in Prestonburg. I wanted to do cartwheels right down Main Street, shouting at every one, "We did it! We did it!" But we had another whole day before our plane reservations home, and for all sorts of reasons we didn't dare let on to anybody what had happened. It must have been the longest day of my life.

I spent most of it in my room, with *Gone with the Wind* and the shoes. Grandpa went out and got a cardboard box from the hardware store to put the metal box and shoes in. He also brought back a tin of black shoe polish, and he and Jason spent well over an hour polishing the shoes. By the time they were finished, they almost looked like something you could put on your feet, though the insides were still pretty horrible.

Grandpa and Jason then went about their normal business in town, flirting and skateboarding. What a pair of show-offs! I was terrified that Jason would let something slip to somebody. Grandpa had pointed out that if anybody knew, we could have serious problems. They might try to take the shoes away from us, either by plain old theft or some kind of tricky legal maneuver. After all, we'd found them on public land, and we had no way of proving they really belonged to us.

So I ate cookies and read in my room throughout the day. Every fifteen minutes or so, I'd get up, open the box, and stare at the shoes for a while, particularly at the jewel buttons.

There were twenty-four of them, twelve on each shoe. Nine rubies, five emeralds, ten diamonds. Of course we didn't know for sure that they were real, but it seemed almost certain. Grandpa had gotten out his portable shaving mirror and used one of the diamonds to make a little scratch on the glass. He thought the gems were at least a carat apiece, and some of them were much bigger.

Mid-morning, he and Jason drove clear back to the airport to find a pay phone and call first Dad and then Mom to share our amazing news. We didn't want to take any chances of being overheard by anybody in Prestonburg. I would have liked to go with them, but I really wanted to stay and guard the treasure.

I was terrified that Miss Farnsworth would find the shoes or the metal box while snooping around in my room—she had the looks of a major-league snoop—so I simply never left the room, except to go downstairs for lunch and dinner. And there I could keep an eye on her every second. The shoes were locked in my suitcase during meals, and I made my own bed so she wouldn't have any excuse to be in the room.

Finally the sun set, but I didn't sleep very well that night. I kept dreaming about Langley Patterson and high-button shoes and a mystery woman named Anna, and I kept waking up. Each time I did, I checked on the shoes.

At last it was morning. We packed the shoes in my carry-on bag for the plane, and Grandpa sealed the metal box in the cardboard one. We'd check that, and frankly I didn't care if the airlines lost it.

And then we were back in Marshfield, and I had never felt so happy to be there before. Grandpa had left his car at the airport, so we didn't see Dad and Carolyn until we got back to the house. I don't think they really believed it was true until we set the shoes out on Carolyn's dining table.

They stared at them, as stunned as we'd been when we first saw them.

We'd begun to realize just how complicated it was going to be explaining where they'd come from. The Indian mound would have to remain our secret. If we ever tried to explain to anyone about finding them on national park land, the government would probably snatch them up and we'd never see them again.

But clearly they were ours, and Dad was already talking about appraisals and declarations for inheritance tax. As far as the tax people were concerned, he said, we'd just tell them the jewels were in the secret drawer of the desk.

Which, in a very roundabout way, they had been.

The real story was ours alone. And it was a story of more than just finding a treasure, although I still had an image of myself behind the wheel of a red convertible, and I'm sure Jason still pictured himself slumped in front of his massive TV set. Maybe those things would happen, and maybe they wouldn't.

What *had* happened, though, was something rare and powerful, more rare and powerful than even the reward of the treasure.

We had set out to do something that seemed nearly impossible. And we worked at it, really worked at it, for weeks. When we ran into dead ends, we found our way out of them and tried a different approach. We got discouraged, but we kept on. And in the end, we triumphed.

The feeling of glorious victory was beyond anything I would have ever dreamed possible.

COMPLETE TEXT OF THE LETTER FROM LANGLEY PATTERSON

TO BE OPENED UPON MY DEATH BY THE SURVIVING MALE DESCENDANTS OF LANGLEY PATTERSON, ESQUIRE

Oh, knowledge is a fleeting thing
  Possessing Such makes one a king.
When man has ended worldly strife
  Oh, still goes on most glorious life.

When Heavenbound our spirits climb
  Our earthly wealth is left behind.
But have ye knowledge, heir of mine,
  You shall my hidden treasure find.

The Labyrinth of my design
  Became my son's prison, and mine.
Away we flew, his wings did melt
  My name's fourth letter will you help.
                (DAE **D** ALUS)

She headed west, with lover bold
       In search of California gold.
Her journey's tale a song became
       Third letter of that lady's name?
                (BE **T** SY)

A lady rising from a shell
       Has made the world my praises tell.
Florentine art owed much to me
       My name's fifth letter will help thee.
                (BOTT **I** CELLI)

My properties make special food
       From something which itself is good.
A young one dies and that is how
       My third will help your progress now.
                (RE **N** NET)

The man who built the cotton gin
       Did help the South its fortune win.
But 'twas the North from whence he came
       Second letter of his home state's name?
                (M **A** SSACHUSETTS)

When no white man lived in this county
       A settler came to seek his bounty.
Plantation owner he became
       First letter of his wife's first name?
                (**H** OPE)

No polecat I, I tried to be
       An honor to Commander Lee

Abroad returned from whence I came
        Last letter of my final name?
                (POLIGNA **C**)

One moon has earth, a sight of glory
        Bold Jupiter's a different story
Its moons shine bright while here we slumber
        The second when you write their number?
                (F **O** UR)

The Carolina Parrot flies
        Aloft in Mississippi skies
The color of his head is true
        Its final letter one more clue.
                (YELLO **W**)

I start as pink, but change my hue
        To purple as my life is through
Then pink once more, a final time
        My second letter place in line.
                (?)

Twelve brothers we in ancient day
        And one of us was sold away
One of our names had seven letters
        Its fourth will make your fortune better.
                (ZEB **U** LON)

Though Vivarini painted here
        My fame results from something clear.
Drop it down and it will shatter.
        My first letter is the one to matter.
                (**M** URANO)

A grievous error made I when
      Cordelia's love I failed to ken.
The bard preserved my tragic tale.
      Take my third and you won't fail.
          *(LE **A** R)*

You've solved these puzzles, knowledged one?
      Your work is very nearly done.
Now take these letters you have found
      And move them carefully around.
A name they'll make in proper order
      A site within the County border.
There stand and look round thoroughly
      And find two giant live oak trees.
Walk 'tween them then, your paces measure.
      At 118 there lies the treasure.
There find a small and hidden hole
      When you away a large stone roll.
Your knowledge served you well, my son—
      Your days of wealth have now begun!

ARE YOU ALONE ON PURPOSE?

by Nancy Werlin

Fourteen-year-old Alison Shandling has enough on her hands with an autistic brother and pressure to be a perfect student. Harry Roth's cruel comments about her brother certainly don't help.

But then Harry is seriously injured in a diving accident, and Alison finds herself helping him through his tragedy.

This first novel is a story of two people finding friendship when they thought they had nothing in common except frustration.

LIFE RIDDLES

by Melrose Cooper

Janelle wants to be a writer, but who would want to read about a poor family that just had the electricity turned off, or about a kid who never sees her dad?

There are some things in life Janelle can't figure out—her aunt calls them "life riddles." But as she writes about her family's problems and her own sad and mad feelings, she discovers she *can* make poetry out of pain....

KICKS

by Janet Fitch

Laurie wishes she could be more like
Carla: rich and wild, with a mother
who doesn't care what she does on
her free time.

Soon Carla is hanging out with a
drug-dealing biker crowd, and
Laurie begins to realize how empty—
and risky—Carla's life really is.